SONGS OF POWER

HILARI BELL

Hyperion
New York

For information address Hyperion, 114 Fifth Avenue,
New York, New York 10011-5690.
Printed in the United States of America
First Edition
1 3 5 7 9 10 8 6 4 2

The text for this book is set in 12-point Janson Text.

Library of Congress Cataloging-in-Publication Data

Bell, Hilari.
Songs of power / Hilari Bell.
p. cm.
Summary: Someone is trying to sabotage the underwater habitat where
Imina, the granddaughter of an Inuit shaman, lives after terrorists
have infected the earth's food supply, and Imina must call on her
still undeveloped magical skills to save the colony.
ISBN 0-7868-0561-7 (trade).—ISBN 0-7868-2487-5 (library)
[1. Underwater exploration—Fiction. 2. Magic—Fiction.
3. Inuit—Fiction. 4. Science—Fiction.] I. Title.
PZ7.B38894So 2000
[Fic]—dc21 99-36645

This book is dedicated to my family, who have given me love and support, always.

⁓⁓⁓⁓⁓

A first book requires many acknowledgments. To Sveta Yamin, who gave me invaluable information about Inuit shamanism. To Craig Cooper of the Aquarius Project, for information about saturation diving. To Brad Evenson and Mike Graham, for technical advice on the habitat. To Irene Kraas, my agent, who kept trying for me. To Julia Richardson, my editor, who not only saw the potential of my story, but helped me realize that potential. To the Denver Science Fiction Writers' Guild, the Wild Women Writers of the West, and especially Kara Anne Schreiber, for endless assistance over the hard parts. Without these people, this book wouldn't be what it is, and they all have my deepest thanks.

CHAPTER 1

THERE WERE ONLY FOUR OF THEM *when the council of Makers first met. A perfect circle of seven would have been better. A powered circle, twenty-one, better still.*

"I had hoped for more," the Eldest admitted. "But a quorum is sufficient to make the decision. How say ye, peace or war?"

"War."

"War."

The Young-one hesitated, but agreed. "War."

"War," the Eldest finished. "Thus it is decided. Let us raise our voices in the spell-of-binding-intent."

Imina stared at the blank computer screen in front of her. Today was the deadline to come up with a science

1

project, and she didn't have any idea what she wanted to do. In fact, she didn't want to do a science project at all. She glanced at the wide window—a stingray rippled past.

The windows were one of the few things she liked about the habitat. She never tired of the sea, even when nothing moved through the water. In the two months she'd been here, she'd become accustomed to the round, gray glass walls. At first she'd felt as though she were living in half a pearl.

"Taking the pressure down another two marks," Lisette told her computer. "That's five hundred feet, right?"

Imina's wandering gaze caught the grimace that crossed Ivan's face as he bent over his own screen, and she deduced that it wasn't five hundred feet. She grinned. At least she wasn't the only one Lisette was distracting. Lisette's terminal was on straight record mode, so it wouldn't correct her. It also logged every word of the stream of gossip she aimed at Reba. ". . . I'd heard Dr. Pennyfeather was bent, but nobody told me he was that weird! When I showed him my splinter, he reached into the open access, picked up a sea urchin and put it on my hand, and it started to suck!"

Lisette pushed a button, and a buzzer sounded. Her long sleeves drifted over the controls. Her long fair hair drifted everywhere, a sharp contrast to Reba's short red-brown curls. Imina liked the loose coveralls that were fashionable now; they had lots of pockets. But everything Lisette wore was exaggerated in some way. She should have looked ridiculous in those trailing sleeves, but she didn't. Lisette looked good in anything.

Imina sighed and looked around the half-sphere of the classroom. The younger kids on the other side had only terminals built into their small mobile desks. The older kids had their own computer stations attached to the curving wall, which left the center of their half of the room open for the teacher, or for holo-images. Dr. Sandoval's dark head was bent over Daud's station. They sounded like they'd be busy for a while, so Imina spun away from the accusing blankness of her screen to watch the mouse in the pressure tank open his cage door.

Imina liked the mice. Teaching them to open the door when the buzzer sounded had been Lisette's last science project. Now she was "discovering" whether changes in atmospheric pressure would affect their reflexes or intelligence. It wouldn't, of course. Everyone in the habitat was proof of that, since they lived at the same pressure as the ocean around them. If it didn't affect the scientists, it wouldn't affect the mice. On the other hand, Lisette had her science project working, and Imina didn't even have an idea.

The mouse pulled the ring and scampered through the open door to snatch up his treat. When the door sprang shut, another treat dropped into the cage where the previous treat had been.

"Five point three four seconds," Lisette read the display to the computer. "And when I said I didn't want *creatures* sucking on me, he said he'd be honored to suck it out himself, but he had more germs!"

Reba laughed obediently, and Lisette turned the dial two more marks. "Six hundred feet," she said, pressing the buzzer. "He was a little slower than last time. Maybe it is affecting him."

Ivan turned from the complex lines and squiggles that covered his computer's screen, a serious expression on the long, thin face that went with his long, thin body. Everything about Ivan was serious, from his straight, plain brown hair to the soles of his plain brown shoes. He was using both the keyboard and a stylus, instead of voice-activated mode, Imina noticed. Show-off.

"Have you instructed the unit to alter the mixture of breathing gases to compensate for the pressure?" he asked Lisette.

"Uh, I assumed it did that automatically," Lisette told him. "What does it matter?"

"It matters," said Ivan, "because if you don't have enough helium in the breathing gas, nitrogen will gradually accumulate in the mouse's body, causing disorientation and—"

"He is acting sort of funny, Lisette," said Reba,

gazing into the tank. "Maybe you'd better . . ."

Lisette's cheeks flushed with anger. "All right, then." She spun the dial to zero.

For a moment Imina saw everything in slow motion—each click of the dial under Lisette's hand, the way Reba's eyes widened. Then Ivan leaped forward, knocked Lisette's hand away, and returned the pressure to where it had been.

"You twit," Imina snapped. "You almost killed him!"

"I did not! What do you mean?"

"What's going on here?" Dr. Sandoval hurried to the pressure tank, a harassed expression on his handsome face. At least, Lisette said he was handsome. Imina wasn't so sure. He was a small, neat man, but his features were almost too even. Bland. He didn't look bland now; he looked like an angry teacher. "Can't I leave you kids for five minutes without someone starting a fight?"

The little kids on the other side of the room were staring. Mrs. M'Barra, the humanities teacher, called their attention back to her. Their "revised one-room classroom" could be pretty distracting. On the other hand, it enabled two teachers to switch back and forth with ease, educating all of the small handful of kids who lived in the habitat.

"It was them." Lisette's eyes filled with abused tears. "I was doing my experiment, and he hit my hand, and she started insulting me, and . . ."

"Hush." Dr. Sandoval turned to Reba. "What happened?"

"Lisette turned the pressure down to zero," Reba told him. Her voice was solemn, but her eyes sparkled with excitement. "Ivan knocked her hand away, and Annis called her a stupid twit, and then—"

"Thank you. I see." Dr. Sandoval sighed. "Lisette, you know you can't go from high pressure to lower pressure immediately. That's why, when you dive out of the habitat, you wear a wrist gauge that warns you if you rise too high."

"But that's outside. I thought that in the tank . . ."

Dr. Sandoval shook his head.

Imina snickered.

Lisette flushed. "Well, anyway, she had no right to yell at me like a savage."

Imina's fists clenched. "Which takes more intelligence?" she demanded. "To survive in a brutal environment with only the tools you can devise out of a handful of bone, stone, and hide, or to just *exist* in a . . . a cocoon of technology? Your people couldn't survive in the Arctic till the twentieth century. Mine had—"

"Annis, that's enough," Dr. Sandoval interrupted.

Imina grimaced. She hated being called Annis.

"We all know how proud you are of your heritage,

but science class isn't the place to express it. Get back to work, all of you."

Ivan had already returned to his station. Imina went back to hers and gazed at the blank screen as Dr. Sandoval explained depressurization sickness to Lisette. Why did the silly twit think you had to spend three days in the depressure rooms before you could return to the surface? For fun? A person that stupid shouldn't be allowed to care for an animal. In fact . . . A slow grin spread over Imina's face. Dr. Sandoval had set the pressure tank to decompress the mouse at a safe rate. He hadn't been at high pressure long, so it would be only a few hours till he was ready to return to the cage on the counter where his five companions played.

That cage had the same kind of release mechanism as the trick cage, with an extra latch to keep it closed when the mice played with it.

Imina got up and strolled casually down the arc of the long lab bench that spanned a quarter of the wall. She often watched the mice run in the spinning wheel of their exerciser. She glanced around—no one was watching. The flick of a single finger freed the latch. She wandered back to her computer and turned it slightly, so that her back was to the class when she faced it.

Now for the fun part.

Imina took a deep breath and let it out slowly. All

the surface worries, the nagging thoughts, the distractions, went out with that breath. Another breath. Another. She listened for her pulse, and soon she could hear it. She focused on the steady throb until the outside world vanished, and she was at home in the darkness of her own mind. A light trance only, but good enough.

Come, little brothers, she called the mice. *White fur, small paws, quiver whiskers. I know you. White fur, small paws, quiver whiskers. I know your spirits. I call to your spirits. I sing to your spirits. Listen to me.*

The rhythmic squeak of the exerciser stopped. They were listening. Good.

You hear the buzzer, little brothers. The door can open. You hear the buzzer. Open the door. Treats outside, little brothers. Open the door. Freedom outside. Open—

She grinned when she heard the tiny snap as the door sprang back. But now what? Imina opened her eyes. She could see the bench clearly, but it was distant, like looking through the wrong end of binoculars. The first mouse climbed out and dropped to the counter. Imina looked for escape routes. A plant at the end of the counter grew happily under an ultraviolet light, its leaves trailing almost to the floor. And on the floor was a vent where Imina had often smelled food cooking. It must lead directly to the cafeteria. Perfect.

Escape, little brothers. Run for the plant. Hide in the

leaves like the wild ones do. Escape, little brothers. Follow
the food smells. Find the food. You are hungry, little
brothers. Find the food. Meshed in her suggestion, the
mice raced for the floor vent as if they were starving.

As the last one dropped through, Imina allowed
the world to come back into focus around her. She
was smiling. It was the first spell she had worked,
except to practice, since she had come to the habitat,
and it had worked perfectly. Grandma Ata would
have been proud of her. Who needed a science project,
anyway?

The lesson had switched to literature. They were
starting English now. Last month had been German,
next would be French. This week it was Imina's turn
to help Mrs. M'Barra with the little kids, while the
older students started reading *Hamlet.*

"You can pick any poem in English," Mrs.
M'Barra told her, "as long as it has enough verses for
each of the kids to memorize one. Do you have any
favorite poems, Annis?"

"Not in English," said Imina.

Mrs. M'Barra sighed and then smiled, producing
dimples in her plump cheeks. Her curly, shoulder-
length hair was paler than Lisette's. "When we do
Amerinds, we'll concentrate on the Inuit, just for
you. But English now, all right? How long do you
need to choose a poem?" She gestured at the rack of

book cartridges and the few old paper books that held poetry in English.

"It doesn't matter." Imina grabbed one of the old books and let it fall open. The poem that started on the left-hand page had about the right number of verses. "I'll do this one," she said. "'Casabianca.'"

Mrs. M'Barra blinked. "Are you sure you don't want to think about that?"

Imina shrugged. "It doesn't matter."

"All white man's poetry looks alike to you?" Mrs. M'Barra grinned.

Imina smiled back in spite of herself. "Yes."

"On your head be it." Mrs. M'Barra waved a hand at the little ones. "Read it to them."

"'The boy stood on the burning deck,'" Imina read in a bored voice. "'Whence all but him had fled; / The flame that lit the battle's wreck / Shone round him o'er the dead.'"

The children's eyes widened. The old-fashioned language made Marinka and Luke giggle. Mrs. M'Barra's lips twitched. A soft chime sounded from the pressure tank on the other side of the room, and Imina's heart began to pound.

Lisette started to rise, but Dr. Sandoval waved her back to her terminal and went to get the cage himself.

"Annis," Mrs. M'Barra prompted. "You're sure you want that one?"

"Ah, sure." Imina went on reading, trying to watch

Dr. Sandoval at the same time. "'Yet beautiful and bright he stood, / As born to rule the storm; / A creature of heroic blood, / A proud though childlike form.'"

The ship burned to pieces and blew up under the wretched boy while Dr. Sandoval pulled the cage from the pressure tank and set it on the counter. Then Reba called him over to answer a question. He said he'd try, though he didn't know much about *Hamlet.*

"'But the noblest thing that perished there / Was that young and faithful heart,'" Imina finished desperately.

All the kids were giggling now, and Mrs. M'Barra gave up the struggle and laughed aloud. "What do you say, kids? Shall we have Annis pick another poem?"

"No!" came the unanimous chorus.

"I want to do the fire verse."

"No, I want that one."

"I want the one where he calls his father."

"There's three of those, you twit."

"I want the first one."

"I want the last one."

"No, I want the last father verse."

"Annis?" Mrs. M'Barra was still laughing.

"Let me think about it."

Imina gazed at the mouse Lisette had been working with, in his cage on the counter. He should be with his friends. There was no time for subtlety, but he'd just been playing with the door. She closed her eyes and willed the raucous blare of the buzzer into his mind. He twitched a little and tried the door. A few seconds later he was out.

She tried to send him down the counter as she had the others, but she hadn't established any real contact with him, and he wandered aimlessly over to his old cage. Mei-lin tugged at her sleeve. "Can I have the first father verse?"

Imina sorted out verses among the children. The mouse was following his friends' scent. Luke was shouting louder than the others, so Imina gave him the verse where the boy got blown to bits. The mouse had almost reached the vent.

"My mice!" Lisette's shriek split the air.

"Run, little brother," Imina shouted. She threw the poetry book at the plant.

The startled mouse leaped for the vent and vanished.

"She did it!" Lisette shrieked, pointing at Imina. "She stole my mice!"

They had sent the children to play in the small, seldom-used gym. Dr. Sandoval and the older kids gathered around the vent. "No doubt about it," he sighed, straightening up. "Those mice are in the cafeteria by now. We'll have to trap them."

He glared at Imina, who promptly resolved to put the evil eye on all the traps so they wouldn't catch anything.

"Did you do it?" he asked.

Imina considered denying it and decided not to.

"I thought I'd start a suboceanic ecosystem," she told him. "The cafeteria should be able to support life. It's my science project."

"What about *my* project?" wailed Lisette.

"It's logical that with her background she'd sympathize with animals," Ivan pointed out. "She probably doesn't—"

"It's better to care about animals than to have a computer crystal for a heart," Imina hissed at him.

"Better that than a brain that stopped in the Stone Age," said Ivan coolly.

"She's a thief," said Lisette.

"Be quiet," Dr. Sandoval snapped. "I'm sick to death of the three of you bickering.

"Annis, since you and Ivan have so little under-standing of each other's point of view, I'm going to have you switch science projects. Annis, I want you to do Ivan's project. He's studying the effects of the earth's magnetic fields on whale migration."

"But I don't—"

"If you don't understand his work, then you'll have to ask his help, won't you? What are you working on?"

Imina opened her mouth, shut it, and opened it again. "Whales." She hated copying Ivan, but it was the only thing she could think of.

"Good, you'll have some common ground. What about whales? Their repopulation? Their physiology?"

"Intelligence," said Imina. "They're probably as smart as we are."

"There is no evidence of that," said Ivan.

"My people know a lot more about whales than—"

"Then Ivan will need your help, too," Dr. Sandoval interrupted firmly, "and maybe you can reach some understanding."

"But what about me?" Lisette looked smug. "All I did was make a simple mistake, and she—"

"Simple-minded," muttered Ivan.

Lisette glared at him. "She ruined—"

"*You* will write a full report on rapid decompression and its effects on mammals," said Dr. Sandoval. The smug look vanished from Lisette's face. "And I want the lot of you to talk with Dr. Kent about the need for cooperation in an enclosed environment. Annis, you can go now. I'll comm her office and make sure she's free."

"You know, Annis, sooner or later you'll have to make peace with the other kids. Have you considered that?"

Imina shrugged.

Dr. Kent was one of the few people in the

habitat who'd taken the trouble to paint her office walls—a warm, soothing cream. Her hair, black as Imina's, was caught up in a knot at the nape of her neck. Her skin was almost the same shade of honey-gold. But Dr. Kent's face was a sculpture of oval lines that made even Lisette look plain. And the psychiatrist was as smart as she was beautiful, which Imina considered almost as unfair as it was dangerous.

Now Dr. Kent sighed. "What would you like to do about your problems with Lisette?"

"Put the evil eye on her," said Imina.

The psychiatrist's brows snapped together. "Really?"

"Of course not," said Imina hastily. "I know there's no such thing as magic. I was only joking."

Dr. Kent's lovely face was still neutral, and a chill ran down Imina's spine. Dr. Kent was so gentle, Imina sometimes forgot she was the enemy.

"You don't joke much, Annis. Didn't you tell me magic was your favorite pretend game when you were young?"

Sometimes Dr. Kent could be distracted by another subject, if Imina introduced it right. "You know, I really hate being called Annis," she said with heartfelt sincerity.

A flicker of interest crossed Dr. Kent's face. "What would you rather be called?"

"Oh, nothing." Imina shrugged. "I just hate my name."

"That's not what you said," said Dr. Kent. "You said you didn't like being *called* Annis." She let the statement lie, but Imina was used to that strategy. She could be silent longer than Dr. Kent could.

You want to be called Imina, tell people to call you Imina, her grandmother had said. *It's only a name.* But to her it meant more than that. Imina was an Inuit name, a shaman's name. And Imina wasn't a shaman, for the spirits hadn't chosen her—yet. Somehow, she couldn't let people call her Imina unless she was sure she deserved it. And there was no one left to teach her magic now that Grandma Ata was gone.

"All right." Dr. Kent gave in. "Let's talk about Lisette. You know how important the habitat is, Annis. In an enclosed environment like this, tension between people can become unbearable. Why do you dislike Lisette so much?"

"She's a twit." Imina scowled. "I mean, she wants to be a model, of all the stupid things."

"She probably doesn't know what she wants to be yet. Not everyone has your strong sense of personal identity."

Imina grinned. "You mean Lisette has a weak identity?"

Dr. Kent shook her head ruefully. "Annis, what

would your grandmother have said to you about Lisette?"

Imina thought for moment, then grimaced. "She would have said that she was too petty to worry about, and that if I couldn't live in harmony with her, I should just ignore her."

"What do you think?"

"I think her identity's so weak, she can't stand to have anyone around who doesn't squirm for her. And I'll bet that before I came, she tried to flirt with Ivan and he ignored her, so she really doesn't like him. Am I right?"

Dr. Kent smiled and shook her head. "Maybe you and Ivan should form an alliance."

"But he's a technocrat," Imina protested. "He talks about nothing but quarks and equations."

"Then maybe . . . Annis, is there someone, anyone here, whom you trust?"

Imina nodded, trying frantically to come up with a name Dr. Kent would believe. But the psychiatrist surprised her. "Then why don't you go to that person, right now if you can, and tell him or her your problems, and let that person help you."

"Thanks." Imina rose slowly. "That's a good idea. I think I will."

Imina fastened the pouch that held her grandmother's shaman belt to her waist. She settled the rim of her full-face diving mask carefully behind her jaw, so the seal wouldn't open when she spoke, and tightened the strap so the cuff rested comfortably behind her ears. She decided not to turn the sonocom on—she didn't want to talk to anyone. She plunged through the open access into the sea. The vibration behind her right ear told her that the miniaturized gill was at work, extracting oxygen from the water around her, releasing the carbon dioxide and recirculating the nitrogen and helium.

The water of the Scotia ridge ran bitterly cold over her hands and through her hair, but when she was just swimming around the habitat, Imina didn't like to bother with hood and gloves. The environmental sensors that adjusted the temperature in her skin suit kept her warm enough for short distances.

Imina swam rapidly past the clusters of spheres that made up different sections of the habitat. She hoped no one was looking out, but as long as she avoided the beam lights that lit the area outside the habitat's windows, there wouldn't be enough ambient light to identify her. She would be just another diver, anonymous in mask and skin suit, heading for the open access at the lower level of maintenance.

The sea life usually gathered around the lights, like moths did on the surface, so Imina was startled when the huge fish rammed into her side. "Stupid!"

she exclaimed in disgust. "Get out of here, Stupid. I don't want you."

The big grouper butted her again, and Imina pushed him away. He swam off about five feet and hovered behind her as she went on. "Other people train dolphins to follow them around, and what do I get? A big, ugly, stupid fish!"

Stupid had attached himself to Imina soon after she'd arrived at the habitat. He followed her on most of her dives. He found her bedroom window and banged against the glass at night until she got up and pulled down the blinds. She dreaded the day he found the windows of the classroom.

Maybe he wouldn't—he really was stupid. Graceful, though. All things in the sea were graceful.

As she swam into the ring of lights that circled the big sphere, the living carpet covering the sea floor became visible in all its color and variety. Imina hadn't wanted to live in the habitat, and she still found the mazelike jumble of round rooms and corridors sterile and unnatural. But from the first, she had loved the sea—the world where the fingerless goddess Sedna lived, with crabs in her drifting hair. Some people felt like they were trespassing when they swam the ocean floor, but for Imina, it felt right. Inuit shamans had been making spirit journeys to Sedna's world for thousands of years; diving gear just made it possible for the body to go along.

A tingle swept over her skin as she swam through the force net. It kept small particles from drifting into the water intakes that supplied the artificial gills that gave the habitat oxygen. The huge, curved wall of the central sphere appeared before her, and Imina swam down beside it and into the vertical tube that led to the lowest open access in maintenance. From there it was only three ladders down to the very bottom of the complex.

Imina pulled herself out of the sea, took off her mask and squeezed the water from her hair. Some people disliked the oil and hot plastic smell of machines, but she liked it—it reminded her of her father.

Imina had been looking for him when she found this place. There were no windows in maintenance. The only reason she'd known she was at the bottom was that the floor curved up slightly all around her. The conduit-covered ceiling was too low for her to stand. Sitting in the hollow of the lowest point in the habitat, Imina had pressed her hands to the floor and felt earth beneath it, not the environmental control machinery that took up the bottom third of all the other spheres.

With earth beneath her and the sea above, Imina had realized that this was the place to work magic. A place where the spirits might come. For ultimately, no matter how hard you studied and tried, it was up to the spirits to choose a shaman.

When Grandma Ata had been called, the fever, the visions, had lasted almost two days, and dozens of spirits had come to her, offering their aid and power.

The spirits hadn't offered Imina the time of day. Yet.

Her wet skin suit slipped on the smooth floor, but Imina had learned the hard way that you couldn't climb down through all the levels of maintenance without some techy grown-up demanding to know what you were doing there.

No one ever came this low. Imina pulled off her belt light and switched it from beam to glow.

Settling into the hollow in the center of the floor, she pulled out her grandmother's belt. The worn white caribou hide was softer than flower petals. The carved horn and bone of the amulets clicked quietly. Sometimes Imina thought she felt her grandmother's presence when she handled the belt. She knew it was there. She had chanted for her grandmother, in that cold hospital room, lending her power for her final spell. "It's right for the conscious part of the spirit to pass on," her grandmother had said, her strong voice so frail that Imina had blinked back tears, "whether you want to go or not. And it's right for the other half of the spirit to be drawn to a new life, bound with your name. But my knowledge, my power, are still needed here."

She had bound both parts of her spirit to this world. But when Imina had tried to summon her spirit, she had always failed. Perhaps now . . . No. No doubts.

Imina took a deep breath and let it go.

"*Aja-ja aja-ja,*" she chanted. "*Aja-ja aja-ja.*"

When Grandma Ata had learned to go into the deep trance, the elders of the tribe had chanted for her. When Imina was learning, Grandma Ata had chanted. Now the machine's whispered chant encompassed the rhythm of hers, so the machines chanted for her, and her heart beat a steady counterpoint to the pulse of the machines.

Her spirit was a core of light, drifting loosely in the darkness of her body, needing only a push of will to separate the two. But a spirit journey was not what Imina sought now. She wanted another's spirit to come to her.

She remembered her grandmother. Sewing, singing, teaching. Her face laughing. Her face severe with concentration. Her face dirty gray with the approach of death. *My task is yet undone. I bind both parts of my spirit to my name, that my power will remain whole after my death. I bind my name to my belt, so it does not stray into other paths. I bind my spirit to my name. I bind my name to my belt.* Then the soft mechanical beep that monitored her heart had become a single-toned cry, and Grandma Ata's spirit was gone.

Now Imina wrapped the power of the trance around the shaman belt and let her grief and loneliness and need well up in a single summoning call.

"Grandmother!"

In the stillness of her spirit, she listened. Nothing. The weary chill of failure spread from her heart into her flesh. If she were a shaman, she could do it. When Grandma Ata summoned ghosts, they thronged about her, so thick Imina had almost been able to touch them. But she had died before she taught Imina to summon the spirits of the dead, and now there was no one to teach her.

The spirits wouldn't choose her. She would never be a shaman. She would learn to call herself Annis, and the part of her that could speak to the minds of mice would die and leave her wandering through the world half-souled. An untrained shaman who could never hear the whispers of the spirit world.

But she did hear something. An unfamiliar song tugging at the edges of the trance. Grandma? No. The odd, irregular rhythm was like no spell she had ever heard. A machine? Imina opened her senses and let the song flow through her. It held will and a fierce intent—will, binding itself with magic. No machine. This was a spell being cast by shamans. But what spell? The words were just beginning to come clear when the song ceased.

Her eyes flew open, and the trance fell away with a suddenness that left her heart thudding. No, not a machine at all. Someone was making magic in the habitat.

CHAPTER 2

"WE SHOULD KILL THEM," *said the Singer. "What have they ever offered our kind but death?"*

"But we are a people of peace," the Young-one protested. "You are proposing that we work black magic!"

"Do we have any alternative?" said the Eldest. "We are the guardians. That responsibility comes before all else."

"They have many lights," the Young-one observed. "Perhaps if we break the lights they will leave."

"Hmm. Can our magic break their lights?"

"Well, there's one way to find out . . ."

But who were they? The last act of *Hamlet* scrolled

slowly over Imina's screen. She'd seen the play, so she was using her lit period to think.

She had to discover who these shamans were. And they might not be shamans—they could be wiccans, or any of a dozen other groups. Every culture on the planet had once had some way to practice magic. But no matter how different their magic might be, surely she could learn from them. Grandma Ata had taught her that all magic was the same at its core. Over the years, as the world she grew up in changed around her, Grandma Ata had changed her Inuit magic to match the world, borrowing from other traditions whenever she felt they had something to offer. And even if these . . . these makers of magic could teach Imina nothing, they'd still be people she could talk to. People who'd believe her and understand. She had to find them.

But how? There were 684 people in the habitat. Her first thought had been to try to find them with magic, but she was afraid it wouldn't work. It was fairly easy to find a person with magic if you knew them, or even had something that belonged to them. But when you didn't have the foggiest idea who they were . . . She didn't even know how to start.

She could put a note on the electronic bulletin board. *All magic makers currently practicing in the habitat, please contact Annis Campbell.* Imina grinned. If Dr. Kent saw a note like that, Imina's craziness would be confirmed for good.

Besides, Imina wanted to find them herself. Her cleverness in discovering them would be proof that she was worthy to be their student. But how? Any techy person who practiced magic would be laughed out of the scientific community . . . and right into mental rehab. Imina shivered.

When Hamlet wanted the King of Denmark to reveal his guilt, he staged a re-creation of the crime. Imina could hardly do that, but . . . If she started a conversation . . . No, just one word. A word only a magic maker would recognize, dropped casually into a sentence. What word?

"Computer," said Imina softly. "Interrupt. Reference mode, thesaurus function. I need a list of really obscure words related to magic."

"I have no uhsarus function," the computer replied, automatically matching the volume of its voice to hers. "Please clarify."

"*The*saurus, twit," Imina muttered.

"Thank you. Working."

The list appeared. Thaumaturgy? Phylactery? Prestidigitator? But that was stage magic. Imina didn't recognize most of these words herself. Would a magic maker who worked in English-amalgam instead of Inupiaq know them? How did she know what language they spoke? Living Planet had people from all over the world working in the habitat.

"Computer, make another list of words, related to real magic, not stage-type magic tricks, and only semiobscure words. Not really common, but not this obscure, either."

"Working."

Necromancy. This was better, but a little hard to work into a conversation. Cantrips. Merrythought. Scry. Scrying? "Computer, define *scrying*."

"Scrying; to see from afar by magic, usually with the aid of a reflective object. From the Old English descry."

Hmm. It sounded like scrying was another version of what her grandmother called Seeing. An English-speaking magic maker should recognize the term. And it wasn't too hard to work into a conversation. I lost my something-or-other. I tried scrying for it, but it didn't work. Have you seen—

"Scrying?" Mrs. M'Barra's soft hand fell on Imina's shoulder and she jumped. "Sorry, I didn't mean to startle you. It's time for you to come work with the kids. I don't remember any scrying in *Hamlet*."

"I, um, I was working on something else."

"*Macbeth*, maybe," Mrs. M'Barra said cheerfully. "Though I'm not sure I'd call that scrying. Maybe a cross between summoning and conjuration."

Imina stared blankly. Mrs. M'Barra? Surely not. And yet . . . she obviously knew something about magic.

"Scrying is a fraud," said Dr. Sandoval. "It has been statistically disproven many times, along with divining and map location."

Mrs. M'Barra laughed. "'There are more things in heaven and earth, Horatio.' That *is* Hamlet. Come on, Annis, the kids are waiting."

The fractious children claimed all Imina's attention. Most of the time she liked the little kids, but today they made her crazy, wiggling and giggling and reciting pieces of each other's verses of the poem. Of course, none of them wanted to work at memorizing their own verses.

Returning to the one-room school was supposed to help them develop a sense of community and responsibility, but Imina let out a sigh of relief when the class was dismissed.

"Maybe if you explained the poem, they'd take it more seriously," said Mrs. M'Barra gently.

"But it's such a stupid poem."

"Not really. The language is a little extravagant, but the story is both sad and heroic. And some of it's beautiful. 'They wrapt the ship in splendor wild, / They caught the flag on high, / And streamed above the gallant child, / Like banners in the sky.' Can't you see that ship burning, Annis?"

"That part's all right," Imina admitted. "It's just that the boy's such a twit. Everyone else has the brains to run. If he was trying to put out the fire, or throw the gunpowder overboard, that would be different. But all he does is stay put because his father tells him to. I think he deserves to get blown up."

Mrs. M'Barra grinned. "But *he* thinks it's important to stay. Important enough to die for. Think about it."

What Imina thought about was Mrs. M'Barra as a magic maker. She wandered slowly in the direction of her family's quarters, stopping occasionally to look out the windows or at a holograph on the wall. Most of them had been taken by habitat residents. Some were awful. She liked the view out the windows better.

At least mentioning scrying seemed to work. She had discovered that both Mrs. M'Barra and Dr. Sandoval knew a lot more about magic than she would have thought.

"Annis!" Imina jumped. Her mother walked toward her from a nearby open access, her skin suit gleaming with water and dozens of specimen jars hanging from her belt. She'd pulled off her hood, freeing straight black hair just like Imina's. "Have you had a hearing test lately? I called you three times."

"I'm sorry. I was thinking about something."

"I know, but most people respond to their names."
She tipped Imina's face up, concern in her slanted
black eyes. Eyes like Imina's. Eyes like Grandma
Ata's.

How can she look so like an Inuit and not be one
of us? Imina wondered for the thousandth time. "I'm
fine, Mom. The school tested everybody a few
months ago. What have you got?" Imina gestured to
the vials hanging on her mother's belt.

Her mother's whole face lit up. "Look at this."
She held a jar of murky water up to the light and
shook it—something flashed iridescently. "The
thickest concentration of zooplankton I've ever seen.
And in late winter, too! It was around the blue
spectrum lights. I need to analyze it, of course, to see
what percentage of phytoplankton is supporting it,
but—"

"That's wonderful, Mom," said Imina. "You do
that."

"I'm sorry, honey." Her mother hugged her. "I
didn't mean to bore you with techy stuff."

"That's all right." Imina tried to put some
enthusiasm into her smile. "I'll see you at dinner."
Her mother hurried off in the direction of the lab
complex, almost dancing as she walked. How could
anyone get that excited over plankton? Plankton was
boring, even if it was going to save the world.

Her mother wouldn't have the foggiest idea what

either Seeing or scrying was. Neither would her father. You couldn't believe in magic and be a scientist at the same time—the mind-set was too different. But everyone in the habitat was a techy person of some sort . . . almost everyone. Imina hurried to her room and went straight to her desk terminal.

"Computer on. Computer, give me a list of all the people in the habitat who don't have an advanced degree in any hard science or engineering field."

"Working."

Twenty-two names washed onto the screen. All the kids, of course. Forget the little ones. Could any of the older kids be magic makers? Imina was. But Imina was only half-trained. The spell she'd felt had been complex—powerful. No, there were adult magic makers behind that spell.

"Computer, eliminate all the people on that list who are under eighteen years old."

"Working." The screen blinked. Eight names remained.

1. Lana Balinski
2. Eloise Bouchard
3. J. D. Hoenstauffen
4. Dr. Andrea Kent
5. Darru M'Barra
6. Marian M'Barra
7. Dr. Giles Pennyfeather
8. Dr. Ricardo Sandoval

Lana Balinski. Of course! Ms. Balinski was an artist who had come to the habitat to paint underseascapes. She might very well be one of the magic makers.

Eloise Bouchard was Lisette's mother. Well, that didn't mean she couldn't make magic. She ran the cafeteria—Imina could ask her about scrying this afternoon. And Ms. Balinski was giving the older kids an art class tomorrow, so it would be easy to ask her, too.

J. D. Hoenstauffen. "Computer, who is J. D. Hoenstauffen?"

"Mr. Hoenstauffen is a physical therapist and gymnastics and sports instructor. He has a B.A. in—"

"All right, that's enough. Go back to the list."

He must be the guy with all the muscles who took care of the gym. Most people never went to the gymnasium. Because they lived in constant contact with the ocean, humidity in the habitat was always high, despite the sophisticated environmental control equipment that struggled against it. Anyone who exercised immediately started sweating like a pig. And why exercise inside when you had an ocean to swim in? But there was no reason he couldn't be a magic maker.

Dr. Andrea Kent. Dr. Kent's degrees were in psychiatry, which was almost a techy subject. And just mentioning magic to Dr. Kent was likely to get Imina shipped off to mental rehab. A chill passed down her spine at the thought. No, not Dr. Kent.

Mr. M'Barra, next on the list, was the administrator in charge of the habitat. Imina had met him when she first arrived—his thin, intellectual, black face and reserved manner intimidated her. She'd also known that he had to have read the hospital's report that she was crazy, so she hadn't wanted to say much. But he'd been nice, in a remote sort of way. And Mrs. M'Barra loved him, so he couldn't be too bad. But the head of the habitat a magic maker? Probably not.

Mrs. M'Barra was another matter. She and Dr. Sandoval had both proved they knew something about magic.

Dr. Sandoval was . . . difficult. His doctorate was in education. He was the one who'd reinvented the one-room school for the habitats, and Imina often wondered if he regretted it, since he'd committed himself to teaching in one to test out his concept. But he had undergraduate degrees in science. He was a techy person. Still, he knew what scrying was.

Dr. Giles Pennyfeather. Imina had never met him because she hadn't been sick since she'd arrived. On the other hand, anyone Lisette thought was "bent" was probably a good candidate.

Now to ask them her question. If she hurried, she could probably talk to Mrs. Bouchard before her parents came home for dinner.

〰〰〰〰

The cafeteria was one of Imina's favorite rooms in the habitat. The round tables echoed the round walls, and the whole upper part of the big sphere was transparent; the glowing grow lights that encouraged the climbing vines drew shoals of curious fish.

"Hello, *petite*. You are my daughter's classmate, Annis, aren't you?" Mrs. Bouchard had to shout over the clatter of the big machine that was sorting the lunch dishes into the recycler. She threw up her hands and gestured for Imina to follow her through a soundproofed door into her office, just off the big kitchen. "Yes, you are Annis Campbell. You look *very* like your mother." She smiled. She wasn't nearly as pretty as Lisette, but her face had a comfortable, lived-in look that Imina liked. "You have some complaint about the food?"

"Oh, no, it's great. Always." It was. "It's just that I lost a pin a few days ago. Ivory, carved like a seal. I tried scrying for it, but I couldn't find it, and I wonder if I could have dropped it in the cafeteria."

"A carved ivory seal? How beautiful. I'm sorry, *petite*, but I haven't seen it. Have you asked the maintenance people? Perhaps one of those machines that crawl around the halls at night has found it."

Imina left Mrs. Bouchard in her office. She was on her way out of the kitchen when a metal box in the corner caught her eye. There was another beside the storage bins. Mousetraps? She picked one up and peered inside. She didn't know what generated the red beam, but she could tell the trap would close when the mouse passed the electronic eyes. It was baited with peanut butter.

Imina grinned and cast a thoughtful look at the closed door of Mrs. Bouchard's office. The evil eye took only a few moments to cast. These techy traps would catch no mice if she could help it.

She had time for a shower before dinner. As the water rushed over her skin, Imina considered the interview. If Mrs. Bouchard knew what scrying was, she was the best actor who'd ever lived. Scratch one. At least her question seemed to produce results. People either knew, or they didn't.

Tomorrow during art class she'd ask Mrs. Balinski. And in the afternoon, Mr. Hoenstauffen. As for Dr. Pennyfeather . . . She could pretend to be sick, but a doctor might guess she was faking. And there was a better way. Holding her left arm carefully out of the spray, Imina punched the button that flooded the shower water with antibacterial agents. In the high humidity of the habitat, skin rashes were a constant problem. It shouldn't take long at all.

Imina's father hadn't arrived by the time Imina came out for dinner, so her mother sent her to look for him. "I tried comming him, but he doesn't answer, so he's probably involved in something," her mother told her. "Try to find out how long he's going to be, because I'm hungry; and if he's not going to be home for hours, we'll eat without him."

So Imina roved the tangled, windowless corridors of maintenance. She liked the maintenance sphere, with its many-storied jungle of anonymous machines. The few technicians she met seldom spoke, except to tell her where they'd seen her father last. She finally tracked him down in a repair bay, in the west side of the sphere. "Dad! Mom wants to know when you're coming home for dinner, because she's hungry and so am . . . Ah, hello, Mr. M'Barra."

The administrator nodded gravely. "We won't be much longer, Annis," he promised with absentminded politeness.

Her father gave her a swift grin and a wink and went on talking. "What I can't figure out is how it happened." His clean, freckled hand gestured to the cracked face of the huge sun-light. Imina loved her father, but she was glad she'd inherited her mother's Inuit coloring instead of his sparse gingery hair and freckled skin. She'd gotten shortness from both of them.

"If something struck it, the cracks should have spread from the point of impact," her father went on. "But this is cracked all over, almost as if the matrix was shattered by force waves or sonics."

"Could it have been pressure?" asked Mr. M'Barra.

Imina studied him intently. He was even more serious than Ivan. His curly black hair was threaded with gray, though his dark-skinned face seemed too young for gray hairs. He looked more approachable crouched over the light with her father than he had at their formal meeting. Should she ask him about scrying while she had the chance?

"It might," her father said dubiously. "But it held up to the pressure just fine for the last eighteen months. Frankly, it just doesn't look right to me."

"Well, chalk it up to one of life's mysteries, and go have dinner," said Mr. M'Barra. "I'm hungry myself."

Imina made up her mind. "Um, Mr. M'Barra . . ."

"I'm sorry," he said absently. "I haven't seen it. Try maintenance. Sandy, if you get any more odd equipment failures, let me know, and I'll track it back to the factory. It's probably nothing, but the habitat project is too important to take chances with."

"Sure." Her father nodded. "Come on, lassie. Let's go rescue your poor starving mum."

Imina followed her father down the corridors, silent with shock. She went over the incident again in her mind. There was no way around it—Mr. M'Barra had answered her question before she'd asked. Did that mean he was a magic maker? He might just be psychic. Grandma Ata thought a shaman had to have a strong parapsychic talent, even though she and Imina never came out better than average on the tests for psychic ability. She said they tested for the wrong things. Maybe Mr. M'Barra wasn't a magic maker, but he had certainly added himself to the list of possibles.

Imina scratched her arm. At her art lesson tomorrow she'd check out Ms. Balinski. That intense, exotic woman just had to be a magic maker. She hoped.

Ms. Balinski had never heard of scrying, nor had Mr. Hoenstauffen. So that left Mr. and Mrs. M'Barra and Dr. Sandoval still possibles, with Dr. Pennyfeather an unknown. Imina thumped her pillow and sighed. She'd be able to check him out tomorrow. The rash had appeared on the inside of her arm that evening, but she hadn't told her parents. She wanted it to be really convincing when she went to the doctor. It itched like crazy. She'd smeared salve on it before going to bed, so it itched less now, but she still couldn't sleep. They said the diagnostic equipment buried in the mattress was undetectable, but on nights like this Imina swore she felt it prickling through her body as it monitored all her vital signs to be sure she was adapting properly to the pressure.

Just because they knew what scrying was didn't mean they made magic. Maybe these magic makers were hard-core technocrats, crouching somewhere in maintenance and working all their spells by computer. Imina thumped her pillow again. Maybe she should call them magically. Why not?

She jumped out of bed and lifted the floor hatch over the cupboard where she kept her most important possessions. When she had first come to the habitat, she'd found it odd that the closets and cupboards were under the floor. But in a room with spherical glass walls, under the floor was the logical place for storage.

She reached down and pulled out her amulet, a small pouch made of the soft, white caribou hide that brought good luck. Her grandmother had made it for her when she was born. In the old days, she would have worn it always. But it made a bulge under her skin suit, and she had been reluctant to have people asking questions about it.

She could feel the small objects inside—a scrap of leather from a bear's jaw for courage, and bone from a fox's skull for cleverness. The shard of an old stone lamp for the warmth of the human hearth. Home. But nothing to increase the power of her magic. Grandma Ata had said she'd be powerful enough on her own. Imina sniffed and wiped her eyes. She took the first deep breath. *"Aja-ja aja-ja."*

It took longer here than in her hideout at the bottom of maintenance, but eventually her spirit floated freely in her body. *Makers of magic*, it whispered, *I am seeking you. I want to find you. I need to find you. Brothers in magic. Sisters in spirit. Answer me. Answer me.*

She felt the song fall away from her, moving out through the habitat and into the sea around it.

She listened. Nothing. Begin again. *Makers of magic, I am seeking you. I want—*

Thump!

Imina jumped and her eyes flew open.

Thump! Thump!

She stared at the window. Two huge fish eyes stared back. "Stupid! Curse you, Stupid!" But she didn't say it twice, even though her heart was still pounding as she snapped down the blind. Words spoken twice had power. She glanced at the amulet, gripped in her hand, but her will to work magic was gone. Oh well. At least she felt more like sleeping. And she could try the scrying question on Dr. Pennyfeather in the morning before school.

"That's quite a rash, m'dear. You should have come sooner." Dr. Pennyfeather reminded Imina of a badger as he poked among the stacks of petri dishes on the cluttered counter. He was tall and thin instead of short and stocky, but he had the same streaky gray and brown hair and the same air of being wholly involved in his own business. "Here we are." He lifted the lid from a dish of blue stuff and sniffed it. "Ah, yes. Decidedly."

Imina hoped he had the right one. He took Imina's wrist gently, pulling her arm straight to expose the rash.

"What is it?" asked Imina.

"Poison, of course," said the doctor.

"Poison!" She jerked her arm away.

"Oh, not to you. At least, not smeared on your arm. I wouldn't recommend swallowing a large amount. But it's absolutely lethal to the critters who are obeying everybody's favorite commandment all over your elbow."

"What commandment?"

"Why, be fruitful and multiply." He took Imina's wrist and examined her arm. "A thriving metropolis, if I do say so." He pushed the petri dish toward Imina. "Do you want to play Godzilla, or shall I?"

"Uh, no thank you."

He scooped up a bluish glob and smeared it over the rash. "A tidal wave of poison jelly engulfs the peaceful city. Ahhhh! The populace panics! The authorities are helpless! This is a job for superfungus!"

Imina began to giggle. Then she laughed so hard she staggered into the wall and sank down against it.

Dr. Pennyfeather washed his hands. "That's a callous way to respond to the death of thousands, I must say."

"You really are bent."

He smiled serenely. "Do you know where that tidal wave of death came from?" He went over to an open access at the far side of the clinic, Imina trailing behind him. The med lab's open access was only a few feet above the sea floor. "See that puffy-looking, purple sponge down there? That's the source."

Imina gazed at the enormous variety of sea creatures that littered the area around the access. "Some of these . . . You imported some of these, didn't you?"

"That's right." Dr. Pennyfeather beamed. "My own personal equivalent of a medieval herb garden. I tried to plant them in beds—starfish in one section, urchins in another—but they kept moving about on me."

Looking at an angle Imina could see that his "garden" extended for many yards, covering the sea floor with a mosaic of colors. "Why not use force nets?" she asked.

"Force nets contain only things that can't move by themselves. And although I know that plankton is the lowest step of the food chain, without which no life is possible, I find it rather boring. This, on the other hand . . ." He gestured proudly at his garden. "I've extracted many of the medicines I use here from these sea creatures. Of course, most of them are still in the experimental stage."

Imina winced. "Including the stuff you put on my arm?"

"Oh, don't worry, m'dear. I'm quite sure that's all right. At least, almost sure. You see those little silver fish in the cold tank over there? Do you know they produce a natural antifreeze that can be used in the treatment of kidney stones? It's a fact." He beamed at her.

"Dr. Pennyfeather?" A woman stood in the door, cradling a swollen wrist against her body.

"Ah, another patient. A busy morning for me, more's the pity. Use the antibacterial in your shower, m'dear, and you'll be all right. And come back to see me someday when you don't itch. You have a very pleasant laugh."

He was walking away before Imina remembered. "Dr. Pennyfeather, uh, have you ever heard of scrying?"

"Of course. But it never worked well for me. Good-bye, m'dear."

Imina wandered slowly toward the classroom. Her arm had almost stopped itching. She hoped Dr. Pennyfeather was a magic maker. Oh, she hoped it. He'd be a wonderful teacher. But in his case, knowing about scrying wasn't conclusive. He might not have a magical bone in his body and still have tried scrying just because . . . because he was Dr.

Pennyfeather. Imina grinned. He probably had a cupboard full of crystal balls.

Imina stopped, gazing absently at a shoal of yellowtails swimming maneuvers outside the window. Any of them might have magical paraphernalia in their cupboards. Imina thought of her grandmother's shaman belt, her amulet, and the omen bones she'd just begun to learn to use. All safely stored under her bedroom floor. Would she recognize the tools of a non-Inuit shaman if she found them? Maybe. And if she found something in their rooms, it would be proof, instead of just a clue like the scrying question.

The M'Barras, Dr. Kent, Dr. Sandoval, and Dr. Pennyfeather. She had to search their quarters.

CHAPTER 3

"THE YOUNG-ONE THINKS SHE HEARD *the call of another Maker,*" said the Great-mother nervously. "*I heard nothing, but my talent doesn't lie in that direction. The Eldest heard nothing either. Did you—*"

"*Yes.*" The Singer brooded. "*The Young-one is right. There is a Maker amongst them.*"

"*But that's impossible! That means . . . The Young-one is already disturbed that we are working the black spells. If this Maker is heard again . . .*"

"*It won't be,*" said the Singer. "*I will cast the spell-of-silence upon this Maker. As long as I maintain it, the council will not hear its voice again.*"

"*Will the Eldest consent to this?*"

46

"It does not need his consent. As Singer, I can cast this spell without help, though it will be weaker than if the circle was with me. It will be stronger if you help."

"The spell-of-silence is far reaching," said the Great-mother uneasily. "It may affect other spells this Maker works. They might discover us."

"Do you fear them?" the Singer asked contemptuously.

"Yes." The Great-mother shuddered. "Those idiot-songs disturb me, and . . . Yes, I fear them."

"Then help me silence their Maker," said the Singer, "or we may have cause to fear."

⁓⁓⁓⁓⁓⁓

"I'm all right, Mom." Imina pushed her pancakes around on her plate. She'd get something from the snack machine outside the cafeteria later—if her plan worked. "I just feel kind of funny. It's probably just the rash." She held up her arm. The itching had stopped during the night, but the roughened skin, dyed blue by Dr. Pennyfeather's "poison," was beginning to peel. It looked awful, but she knew if she suggested staying home, her parents would resist. If she could get them to suggest it . . .

"Oh dear. Do you want to go back and see Dr. Pennyfeather again?" her mother asked.

Imina sighed. "Not now. I just feel sort of tired. Maybe later, if I don't feel better. But it's so embarrassing to have to leave class. Everybody stares at you. I'll wait till after school." She sighed again.

47

Her mother came around the table to feel her forehead. "You aren't hot," she said, "but that doesn't mean much."

"If she says she can go to class, why don't we let her? It's Friday. She'll be home tomorrow anyway." Her father's voice was gently reasonable. Imina cast him a startled glance. He was looking straight at her, eyebrows lifted. Did he know what she was doing? She blushed.

"No, she's a little flushed," her mother said reluctantly. "Would you like me to stay home with you?"

"No!" Imina exclaimed.

Her father choked on a sip of tea and began to cough.

"I mean . . . really, Mom, you don't need to do that. I'll be fine. I just need to take it easy, that's all." Her mother spending the day with her was the last thing she needed.

"Are you sure? You really are flushed, honey." Her mother felt her face again.

"I'll be fine, Mom. I think it's mostly because I didn't sleep much. Because of the itching. I'll just go back to bed and read, and maybe sleep a little." With any luck, that would prevent her mom from checking on her. "Your work is important. How would you feel if there was a worldwide famine because I had a rash?"

"Come on, Signy. If the lassie wants to stay home a day, we can let her. I'm willing to trust her judgment." Her father gave her another straight look.

"Thanks, Dad," said Imina sincerely. Why hadn't she been able to fool him?

Since her parents' work took them all over the world, Imina had seen them only during the rare times between jobs when they stayed with her and Grandma Ata. They'd called on the televid once a week, but they'd always seemed more like friendly guests than parents. He shouldn't have been able to tell she was lying.

"Well, if you're sure." The relief on her mother's face made Imina feel ridiculously guilty—her mother hated to miss work. "But take it easy. No swimming, all right?"

"Sure, Mom. I promise. I'll read awhile and get some sleep." So don't comm me, she willed.

"Actually, Signy, I'm not sure you should be swimming either," said her father. "We've had a couple of whale sightings, and I'm told one of them is a killer whale."

"Whales? That's wonderful," her mother exclaimed. "They're probably attracted by all the plankton."

"Why is it wonderful having whales around to eat your plankton?" Imina asked. "I thought you had to study it and analyze it and stuff."

"Whales are wonderful," her mother repeated, "just because they are. We can spare them a ton or two."

"Killer whales don't eat plankton." Imina's father

began carrying dishes to the recycler. "They eat people."

"There speaks the engineer." Imina's mother grinned. "For your information, they're called orcas, not killer whales, and there have been no reports of whales attacking men since . . . since well before the Worldwide Conservation Treaty was signed."

Imina's fists clenched. The Worldwide Conservation Treaty, which forbade the hunting of any animals not specifically bred for the purpose, had been a death blow to the Inuit way of life. It had happened before her mother was born, but Imina had never quite forgiven her for becoming a member of the political consortium that had been the moving force behind the treaty.

"You mean once we stopped hunting them, they stopped killing people?" her father asked skeptically.

"Of course not. Whales have never attacked people who weren't trying to kill them. It's just that it was about that time, or maybe fifty years earlier, that people started investigating rumors and wild stories and disproving them."

"Besides," said Imina defiantly, "it wasn't the treaty that stopped whale hunting. It was the jinx."

"The what?" Her mother, shuttling back and forth between the table and the recycler, stopped to stare at her.

"Keep an open mind, Signy," said her father.

"Go on, lassie. This sounds good."

Imina wished she hadn't said anything. "Grandma Ata had some friends who worked on the whale boats. A few months before the treaty was signed, there were all kinds of accidents. Fatal ones. Equipment failures. And the whales stopped giving themselves up to the hunters."

"Giving themselves up?" her father asked.

"How could a hunter, in a tiny kayak, with just a spear, kill something the size of a whale if the whale wasn't willing?" Imina asked. "Even later, with big boats, and electric harpoons, how could they find whales in something as big as an ocean if the whales wouldn't come to them? But the whales stopped giving themselves up. Even before the treaty, it was getting hard to find enough men to take the boats out. Otherwise, they would have gone on whaling illegally. The treaty couldn't have stopped them. They were hunters."

"They were hunting their prey to extinction." Her mother's face was cold. "I never understood how Grandma Ata could condone that. She—"

"There speaks the marine biologist." Imina's father interrupted her with a hug. "Go swim with your whales, since you're so sure they're friendly. We're both late."

He put a hand on Imina's shoulder. "Be good, lassie."

The lie stuck in Imina's throat. She hugged him instead. "Thanks, Dad."

"You really don't need me to stay?" her mother asked.

"If I don't feel better after a nap, I'll go see Dr. Pennyfeather," Imina told her. "If there's anything wrong, I'll comm you. All right?"

Once her parents were gone, Imina heaved a sigh of relief. She had the whole day and all her suspects would be in their labs or offices. She gave her parents five minutes, then hurried off to Dr. Pennyfeather's quarters.

Did Dr. Pennyfeather lock his door? Her parents never did. Imina laid her hand on the touchplate and sighed with relief as the door slid open. The computer had given her directions to the personal quarters of all her suspects, but override on a locked door was a different matter.

But why would anyone lock their door? A thief would have to spend three days in decompression before he could escape, and in that time a theft was bound to be discovered. Besides, people in the habitat trusted each other.

Imina pushed the thought aside. "Dr. Pennyfeather?" she called softly. If he was here, she planned to tell him what she had told her parents, but only silence answered. She stepped inside, and the door slid closed behind her. Staring around the cluttered room, she understood how some people felt when they dived. She felt like a trespasser, invading a fascinating world where she didn't belong.

Book cartridges, even some old paper books, and piles and piles of dog-eared printout formed most of the mess. The printout seemed to be mostly medical articles. The book cartridges varied wildly from medical texts to . . .

"*Ratman on Mars?*" said Imina incredulously. She picked up a few more cartridges. The titles weren't conclusive, but . . . She found his reader plate under the pieces of a model of a human skeleton. Full-color capacity. Dr. Pennyfeather read comic books. Imina grinned and slid the reader back under the plastic bones. It looked as if he'd taken the skeleton apart and been unable to put it back together.

Imina opened one of the floor hatches. A wash of paper printout, and sliding down the side . . . a yo-yo? The string was horribly tangled. Imina gave up and went to the first of three doors that led off the main room. It opened into a kitchen, much tidier than the main room or his laboratory. The bathroom was off the kitchen. Imina abandoned the cupboards after a single glance. Nothing out of the ordinary.

A wave of green scent engulfed her when she stepped into the next room. It was filled to overflowing with plants—live plants in pots on stands, bundles of leaves hanging from racks on the ceiling, dried leaves in specimen vials, on shelves that climbed right over the windows. *Chamomile*, Imina began reading the scrawled labels on the pots. *Vervain. Dittony. Small willow.* These were herbs. Herbs could be used for spells.

Excitement flared in Imina's heart. She knelt and pulled up one of the few floor hatches that weren't blocked by racks of heavy potted plants. Mushrooms? But it was. He was growing mushrooms under the floor. Well, why not? Imina let the panel fall closed.

The last room was his bedroom. Here the clutter was even worse. There were several crystals, the natural kind, not crystal balls. And many other odd rocks. And a small skeleton of some animal, intact instead of in pieces. Imina thought it might be a cat, but she wasn't sure.

A bronze model of the Rock of Gibraltar. And a picture. Imina picked it up. It was an old-fashioned 2-D photograph of a much younger Dr. Pennyfeather and a woman. She was holding his arm and laughing; he was smiling at her. His wife? But a woman who looked at a man like that would never divorce him. She must be dead. A wave of guilt swept over Imina. This was something she had no business seeing. She put the photo back and left Dr. Pennyfeather's rooms.

Imina went to the snack vending machine outside the cafeteria and persuaded it to put several gooey buns on her parents' account. It wouldn't have done any good to go on searching Dr. Pennyfeather's rooms. Half the things she found might have been signs of magic. Or, knowing the doctor, they might not. Besides, a really thorough search of those rooms would have taken the rest of the day and half the night. Imina grinned and licked her sticky fingers. Maybe the others' rooms would tell her more.

"Computer, where is Mr. M'Barra?" Imina asked. She wanted to be sure that the M'Barras were accounted for before she searched their rooms. Right now Mrs. M'Barra would be telling the older kids about the empire of Genghis Khan. Mr. M'Barra could be anywhere.

"Mr. M'Barra is in maintenance bay thirty-seven."

"How long will he be there?"

"Unknown."

"Well, what's he doing?"

"Unknown."

"Is any computer terminal being used?"

"One hundred and seventy-two terminals are currently in use in this facility."

Imina gritted her teeth. "Are any terminals being used in maintenance bay, uh, the bay where Mr. M'Barra is?"

"Two terminals are in use in maintenance bay thirty-seven."

"What are they being used for?"

"One is checking factory invoice records. The other is recording into the administration log."

"Can you summarize the information being put into the log for me?"

"Yes. Seventeen ultraviolet sun-lights have been brought in with the shielding glass fractured. Average time in use, fourteen point four months. The chief engineer cannot determine the cause of the damage. Factory invoice records are being checked to deter- mine—"

"Interrupt."

Seventeen lights! That should keep Mr. M'Barra busy for a long time. She hoped. Imina went down the corridor and pressed her hand to the touchplate. The door swished open obediently. Didn't anyone lock their door?

The M'Barras' rooms looked lived in, but they weren't as messy as Dr. Pennyfeather's. The first thing that caught Imina's eye was the music complex. The helium in the habitat's atmosphere distorted sounds—about a fifth of the environmental control equipment was acoustic modifiers. Voices sounded fairly normal, but making music sound like it should was all but impossible, and therefore very expensive. One of the M'Barras must care about music a lot. Mrs. M'Barra? She hadn't talked about it.

Imina rushed through her search of the kitchen

and bathroom. She wanted to get out of here fast, but she didn't want to miss any clues. She was in the bedroom when she heard the swish of the outer door.

". . . want to use my terminal for this." It was Mr. M'Barra's voice. "Maybe I'm being paranoid, but it will only take a few minutes."

The door to the main room was open. Imina dived behind the bed and tried to roll beneath it, but a storage unit filled the space. She crouched behind the bed, her heart pounding. The computer said he was busy! That would teach her to trust a machine. If he came into the bedroom . . .

Another door swished. She listened to the murmur of Mr. M'Barra's voice addressing the computer. He was encoding a message to send to some electronics supply place. But why code? Did it matter if someone saw it?

Finally, he stopped speaking. Imina heard him order the terminal off, then the rustle and grunt people make when they stretch, then his footsteps. They paused at the bedroom door. Imina covered her eyes with her hands. The steps went on and the door swished. Imina's breath whooshed out of her lungs and she sat up. Her hands were shaking.

She was reaching for the door's touchplate when she remembered that she hadn't finished searching. Instinct screamed, "Get out," but she hadn't been caught. Mrs. M'Barra was in class and Mr. M'Barra probably wouldn't come back. This was her best chance. She'd hurry.

The last door off the main room opened into a shared office. It held a few racks of book cartridges, which Imina ignored. There had been book cartridges in the main room and the bedroom, but the titles had nothing to do with magic.

Mr. M'Barra's desk was tidy. He evidently preferred to work on his terminal, for there was very little printout. She glanced at the cold screen, but without his access code it was useless. Imina didn't dare touch much. Tidy people notice when something they work with has been disturbed. Sliding the drawers open she saw nothing that didn't have to do with running the habitat. At the back of one drawer she found diplomas. Mr. M'Barra had a bachelor's degree in biology and a master's degree in business administration. It made sense.

The only thing that didn't make sense was why he had answered a question before she'd asked it.

She went over to Mrs. M'Barra's desk. This was better. Mrs. M'Barra's preference for hard copy was well known. Imina began sorting through the stacks of paper. There were piles of simple exercises from the little kids. And there was her own paper on the rise of civilization in the Orient. She'd gotten a six out of a possible ten. Better than average, but not by much. Lisette had gotten a seven. She grimaced, abandoned the desktop, and pulled open a drawer. The afternoon was passing, and she had to get through Dr. Sandoval's rooms while he was still in class.

The first drawer held ordinary desk junk.

The second was filled with printout, covered with symbols Imina didn't know. At first she assumed it was some sort of equation, but she'd seen her father work with that sort of thing, and this wasn't chemistry or math. "Computer on," Imina whispered.

"Working," the computer whispered back.

"Oh, wait a minute." Imina raised her voice to a more normal tone. She dug through the first drawer until she found a scanner attachment. A wild crisscross of red light bloomed out when she plugged it into the terminal. She ran it over the printout. "Computer, what are these symbols?"

A circle with horns flashed onto the screen. "Taurus." A circle with a cross in the middle. "The Sun." It continued, "Saturn. Pisces. The Moon. Mars."

"Interrupt. What do these symbols mean?"

"Sorry, insufficient data for interpretation."

"I mean, what do the symbols pertain to?"

"These are symbols used in astrology."

Astrology? As in fortune-telling? "Computer, what's astrology?"

"Astrology is the arcane art of determining a person's personality and destiny from the position of the stars, Sun, Moon, and planets at the time of their birth. Now widely disbelieved, it was practiced by the ancient Egyptians, Chinese, Hindus, Etruscans, and Chal—"

"Interrupt. Computer off."

The screen died obediently. An arcane art. It was almost magic. Or was it? All the remaining drawers held astrological printout. Whether it was magic or not, it was something Mrs. M'Barra spent a lot of time on. She believed. "There are more things in heaven and earth, Horatio." Did Mr. M'Barra believe in it, too? Imina would have to find out later. School ended in just two hours, and she still had to search Dr. Sandoval's quarters. At least she didn't have to be so nervous—she knew where he was.

Dr. Sandoval's rooms were cluttered, though not with the delightful chaos of Dr. Pennyfeather's. Models of atoms. Models of the solar system. His desk was in the main room with only two doors off it, almost certainly to a bedroom and kitchen/bath. Imina went over to the desk and began opening drawers. No hard copy, not for Dr. Sandoval.

She glanced at his terminal. He hadn't returned the physics test they'd taken last week, but she didn't really want to know how she'd done. It would only depress her. When she'd first come to the habitat, she'd told Dr. Sandoval that science was against her religion. It was true, but it hadn't worked.

In the bottom drawer she found a small black notebook with hard-copy printing and some hand-written notes. She scowled at the mathematical squiggles. It looked like some kind of puzzle. But why didn't he keep it in his computer like everything else? In any case, it wasn't magic. She shrugged, dropped it back into the drawer, and went to the rack of book cartridges. Science, science, science. *A History of the Seance, Fact and Fraud.* Seance? *Magic and the Paranormal. Statistical Method and the Laws of Chance. Famous Psychics throughout History. Nostradamus and other Prophets.* Imina's jaw dropped. *You Can Learn to Read Auras. Hypnotism and Reincarnation.*

The door swished.

Imina froze for a second, then leaped to crouch behind a big stuffed chair. Peeking beneath it, she saw Dr. Sandoval's shoes enter the room and walk over to the desk. A smaller pair of shoes went with him.

"Computer on. I need a printout of all graded science projects and tests for Daud Ibrahim for the past six months. It seems we have a discrepancy." His voice was dry.

"I know I'm right, Dr. Sandoval," said Daud. "I have at least a seven-point-five average. I'm sure."

Imina cursed soundlessly. Of all the times for Daud to start an argument about his grades! Daud was the only son of brilliant parents, who wanted him to be a scientific genius. Imina felt sorry for him, when she wasn't disgusted by the way he squirmed for Lisette and the teachers. But why couldn't they have done this in the classroom? Oh well. If she was quiet for a just a few more minutes, they'd—

Thump!

Imina jumped and stared in horror at the window over her head. Big blank fish eyes stared back.

Thump! Thump! Thump!

Imina closed her eyes in despair.

"Annis!" Dr. Sandoval's voice was sharp with shock that changed rapidly to anger as he went on. "What the devil are you doing in my room?"

Imina opened her eyes and stood up.

Dr. Sandoval's mouth was tight.

Daud's eyes were wide.

"I asked what you're doing here, young lady."

"Um . . ." *Thump. Thump.* Her mind was blank. What did it matter, anyway? She shrugged.

Dr. Sandoval grabbed her elbow, pulled her from behind the chair, and marched her out of his quarters and down the hall. Imina was aware of Daud watching them go. Lisette was going to love this.

CHAPTER 4

"THE SPELL," *said the Young-one, "is working beautifully. We have broken many of their lights."*

"But they are not leaving," said the Singer. "How many lights must we destroy? This is useless."

The Eldest stirred. "We will destroy as many as it takes to force them out."

~~~~~~~~~~

"I knew she resented it when I made her switch science projects." Yank. "But I never dreamed she'd stoop so low—" Yank. "—as to sneak into my room and try to get some sort of petty revenge."

Imina glared at him. It was a logical assumption for Dr. Sandoval to make, but he didn't have to jerk her arm off.

Dr. Kent rose and laid her hands gently on Imina's shoulders. "I see." She didn't pull Imina away, or even look at the hand that clutched her elbow, but Dr. Sandoval's grip loosened and fell away as she went on. "You have every right to be angry. Why don't we have Annis wait in the outer office while we discuss it?"

She squeezed Imina's shoulders and pushed her out the door. "Wait here," she murmured. "We won't be long."

Imina flopped into a chair. The soundproof door let nothing through, not even when someone yelled. Should she say she had intended to play a trick on Dr. Sandoval? But what trick? She couldn't think of anything she would have wanted to do in Dr. Sandoval's quarters. She was only looking around. She hadn't meant to harm anything.

Imina pushed up her sleeve and examined her elbow. No bruise at all. Rats. She could have used a bruise. She let the sleeve slide down.

Maybe she could say she'd wanted to see the grade on her last test. Without the access code she couldn't have done it, but would they know she knew that?

The door swished open and Imina jumped. Dr. Sandoval glared at her, but he wasn't as angry as he had been. "Tomorrow, young woman, you're going to start that science project." He walked through the outer office and out the door before Imina had time to respond.

"Annis?" Dr. Kent gestured for her to come in and sit down. Imina didn't know what to say, so she said nothing.

Finally, Dr. Kent sighed. "I'm not going to scold you for invading Dr. Sandoval's quarters," she said. "I think I'll let your parents deal with that one. Let me ask you another question instead. How did your grandmother die?"

Imina blinked. That had to be in her personal history. "Pneumonia. At least, that's what they said. She just got sick, and she was so old she couldn't fight it. She would have fought if she could have. She was like that."

"Then that must be where you get it," said Dr. Kent. "Being a fighter. Did you try to fight when your grandmother . . . She was actually your great-grandmother, wasn't she?"

"Yes." Imina nodded. Where was this going?

"Did you fight for your grandmother when she was dying?"

"I wanted to get her out of that hospital," Imina burst out. "All those machines and tubes. The drugs made her talk funny. She hated it. That wasn't what she wanted. The . . ."

The spirits wouldn't come to her there. If the spirits had been able to help her, she might have had a chance.

"They should have let me take her home," she finished bleakly.

"I'm inclined to agree with you," said Dr. Kent. "Do you know why they didn't?"

"They thought they might save her." Imina shrugged. "And I'm only fifteen. They said I was too young."

"But they couldn't save her. Did they try?"

"Sure." Imina shrugged again.

"Why couldn't they save her?"

"I guess . . . She was just too old."

"She was one hundred and thirty-four years old," said Dr. Kent. "Do you know what the average life span is?"

"A hundred and something."

"A hundred and eight. And your grandmother was a hundred and thirty-four."

"I know that." Imina glared at her. "I know they tried. There was nothing they could do."

"If they couldn't do anything, what could you have done?"

I *did* do something, Imina thought proudly. I smuggled in her shaman belt. I chanted for her, and lent my power, so she could work her final spell and die the way she wanted to. I did all I could for her.

"You're wrong, Dr. Kent. I don't feel guilty about Grandma Ata's death. I know there was nothing more I could do."

"Then let her go." Dr. Kent leaned forward intently. "You may not see it, Annis, but she clings to you like cobwebs from the grave. She loved you, and she was wise. Would she have wanted that? You have to let her go, if you're going to get on with life."

"I can't." Tears flooded Imina's eyes. "I need her too much." She jumped up and ran from the office.

She stopped crying on the way home, but it didn't help to find both her parents waiting for her.

"I feel like I'm failing you," her mother grieved. "We hardly know each other. Dr. Kent asked us if you had another name; she said you don't like Annis. Would you rather we call you Imina like Grandma Ata did?"

Imina felt her temper stretching. "No, Mom. You named me Annis. You call me that."

"Actually, I named you Annis," said her father. "And a fine Scot's name it is, for a fine Inuit lassie. But back to the subject. I know sometimes it sounds like fun to play a trick on a teacher. I did it a time or two, myself." He grinned. "Too much energy and not enough sense. But Annis, we're all enclosed down here, just the lot of us, bumping into each other. Having privacy in your own room can be very impor- tant. Aren't there things in your room you'd not want other people messing with?"

Imina thought of her amulet and Grandma Ata's shaman belt. She thought of the old 2-D photograph of Dr. Pennyfeather's wife, and her eyes dropped.

"Her culture was different," her father continued gently, "so I don't know what your grandmother taught you about privacy, but—"

"She wasn't a savage!" Imina's eyes snapped up, and she glared at her father. "The Inuit respect privacy. They respect emotional privacy more than white people do!"

"Annis," her mother protested. "You're three-quarters white yourself. I'm glad you're proud of that part of your heritage, but it's only part. Honestly, sometimes you act as if it's two hundred years ago and people won't accept you if you're Native American."

"Of course they accept *you*," said Imina coldly. "You've become one of them." And she exercised her right to privacy by going into her bedroom and shutting the door.

At first she paced the floor, arguing with her absent parents. They didn't understand her. They didn't understand anything, except their precious science. But eventually she argued herself out and faced the truth. They couldn't understand, because she hadn't told them the truth. Not that they'd understand if she did. They'd just tell Dr. Kent she really was crazy. Imina sighed and ran her hands through her hair. They were still her parents. She took a deep breath and went out to make peace.

"You're going through a hard time." Her mother's

eyes were red. "We shouldn't have been so rough on you."

"Just don't do it again," said her father.

"I didn't mean what I said," Imina told them. "I'm proud of what Mom does. Really. Of both of you."

They hugged her.

"Well, I'm glad you don't have too many moral objections to science. As far as I'm concerned you can be as Inuit as you want. There are worse things." Her mother laughed shakily. "I just remembered. When you were little, you wanted to be a shaman when you grew up. The old-fashioned, magic-making kind. Do you remember that? I'm glad you gave it up. I mean, freedom of religion is one thing, but it would be more than a little embarrassing to explain to my colleagues that my daughter is a witch doctor."

"But one with a wonderful respect for privacy from now on." Her father was teasing—unlike her mother. "Right, lassie?"

"Right." Imina unclenched her teeth. "Everyone needs privacy."

Especially people who make magic. Imina froze for a moment, then resumed hugging her parents, but her thoughts raced. The magic makers would need more privacy than they could find in their quarters, where anyone might come in and interrupt them. They'd have to meet somewhere else. A place where no one would stumble across them. They probably stored their things there, too. Imina gave her parents a last hard hug and pulled away, smiling. Tomorrow was Saturday. She would search the empty quarters.

Imina rubbed her grubby hands and stretched. It was afternoon, and she'd gotten through only three of the seven sets of empty personal quarters. Why hadn't she realized that other people might use these rooms for storage?

She shoved the plasti-crate back over the last vacant floor hatch and leaned against it wearily, glaring at the room full of crates. Spare lab equipment and domestic supplies, according to the labels. Fortunately, only two crates had been opened, so she hadn't needed to search inside all of them. A plasti-crate could be resealed, but the weld always left a visible mark. If only they weren't so heavy.

Imina sighed and peeked out the door to be sure the corridor was empty before going on to the next set of rooms. She rubbed her dirty hands again and grimaced. How could there be so much dust in an undersea environment? She'd have to wash in an open access before she went home. On the other hand, one look at the dust told her which crates had been moved recently. If the dust was undisturbed, she didn't have to bother with the hatch beneath it.

She only wished she'd realized that before she'd

moved all the crates in the first two rooms. The dust also told her which rooms had been entered. Unfortunately, it didn't take footprints well enough to tell her what people did there. If you didn't mind the dirt, you could hold a circus in these rooms and no one would know.

She sighed again. She'd been lucky to have the day free. Her mother had wanted to "spend time with her," but she'd been called to some important conference.

The next suite's door swished open, and the lights went on. More crates. Imina took two steps into the room and froze, staring. This room had been used. Recently. She knelt and studied the scrapes in the dust where someone had pushed crates off the floor hatches. No new dust had gathered there, but they might have been moved days ago.

Could this be the room the magic makers were using? But why would they move crates off the hatches and then push them back? And if they didn't want their use of the room to be discovered, why hadn't they swept the floor? Imina studied the random trails of scuffed dust. No. This was the result of someone doing a search very like her own. But why hadn't they searched all the suites? Either they had found what they were looking for, or . . . Imina hurried to the next set of empty quarters and found the same signs of search.

It was the same in the next one.

She opened the door of the next suite, and Ivan let go of a crate and spun to face her. "What are you doing here?" His utilitarian coveralls were grubby and disheveled, his hands as filthy as hers.

"What are *you* doing here?" Ivan a magic maker? Not possible.

He was staring at her hands. "It looks like I've been doing the same thing you have." His long face was thoughtful. "Searching the empty quarters."

They eyed each other suspiciously.

"Look," said Imina, "if you're looking for something, then you're not the person I want." She gestured to the dust tracks by the disturbed crates. "They wouldn't have to search. And that's probably true of whoever you're looking for—it can't be me, because I'm looking, too. I mean—"

"I understand." Ivan ran a hand through his straight, brown hair. "But I still want to know what you're doing here."

Imina shook her head. "I was thinking we might be able to help each other. For instance, I've searched suites 454, 455, and 456. I didn't find anything but plasti-crates and only two had been opened. They had nothing in them except what the labels said they should."

"Was it electronic equipment?" Ivan asked intently. "Chemicals?"

"No." Why would he care about that? "One had laboratory glassware, and the other was sheets and pillowcases and stuff."

"Damn." Ivan scowled thoughtfully. The silence stretched.

"So what did you find?" Imina demanded.

"Oh." Ivan blinked. He hadn't even been thinking about her, the twit. "I found only one open crate. Maintenance stuff. I checked it carefully and that was all it was." He was thinking again.

"Where have you searched?"

"I looked in 457, 8, 9, and now this one, 460."

"So this is the last one."

Ivan nodded. His expression was odd, but Imina had never had much luck reading Ivan's face.

"I'll help you," she told him. "But first, did you check the dust?"

"Dust?"

"Around the crates. If the dust isn't disturbed, the crate hasn't been moved."

A wave of red swept up from Ivan's collar. Imina decided not to tell him how long it had taken her to figure that out. He stepped back and studied the floor around the crates. The only footprints were his own.

"Well." Ivan rubbed his forehead, leaving a smear of dirt. "On to the next stage, I guess."

"What next stage?"

"The computer." Ivan went to the wall, pulled out

the panel that concealed the terminal, and fumbled behind it.

"But the terminals here aren't connec—"

The screen flashed, and strings of characters began to run over its face. "Connection functional," it announced.

"How did you do that?"

"I turned it on," said Ivan.

Imina blushed. He turned to face her.

"I've decided to trust you," he announced. "You've been acting oddly the last few days, but then, you always act oddly. And you might know something, even if you don't know you know it."

Imina opened her mouth, but nothing came out.

"I'm looking for the saboteurs," Ivan continued. "They must be hiding their equipment somewhere, but if it's not in the empty quarters, we aren't likely to find it. Now I'm going to run an all-files computer search. Do you have any idea what to look for?"

Imina's mouth caught up with her brain. "What saboteurs?"

Ivan stared at her. "The ones who are breaking the lights, of— Has something else happened?"

"Not that I know of. But I thought that was just a malfunction—the factory hadn't tested them for pressure right or something."

"All five hundred and twenty-four of them?" Ivan asked.

Imina's eyes widened. "I thought it was only a dozen or so."

"No." Ivan shook his head. "More than a third of the sun-lights are out. They're meeting now to decide whether to release the force nets and let the plankton drift to the fisheries, or to hold it here and hope we can solve the problem. I can't believe you didn't know about it."

Imina shrugged. "Are any other stations having this problem?"

"No, just us. But if we can't find out who's doing it and stop them . . ." He turned to the computer, pushed the button that extruded the keyboard, and began to type.

A wave of concern washed through Imina. Raising plankton might be boring, but she knew how important it was. Ordinarily, plankton grew only in the first hundred or so feet of water, where the sunlight penetrated. Unfortunately, the water richest in the nutrients the plankton needed was on the bottom. When it had suddenly became necessary to feed the population of the world from the sea, scientists had realized that for the sea to produce more fish for people to feed on, they'd have to produce more plankton for the fish to feed on. So the habitat, and hundreds of other plankton-growing stations, were constructed to bring artificial sunlight to the sea floor. So far they'd been successful.

But if they failed . . . Imina shivered and went over to Ivan.

"What are you doing?"

"Accessing a program in my personal files that will let us access all the computer files."

"But you can't do that. Not unless you know everybody's code."

Ivan shrugged. "It's illegal, but that doesn't mean it can't be done."

"Isn't there some sort of computer security program to stop things like this?"

Ivan looked smug. "This program takes care of that."

"Ready," the computer announced.

"Computer, access all files except library, reference, and news-bank files. Search for phrases . . . Computer, hold." He turned to Imina. "Any ideas?"

"How about Unificationists? If anyone would want to sabotage the habitat, they would."

"I'm afraid it's the right track, but that's too vague." He turned to the terminal. "Computer, search for the phrases; 'all for one and one for all,' 'brotherhood of man,' and 'needs of the many outweigh the needs of the few.' Begin."

"What do those phrases have to do with anything?"

"They're Unificationist catchphrases," said Ivan. "They're outdated, but they're the kind of thing a

Unificationist might use without thinking. If we get a lot of hits in one person's files . . ."

"How do you know them?"

"History books," said Ivan coolly. "This will take a while. Tell me, how are you doing with my science project?"

Technocrats didn't read history. Imina stared at him suspiciously. "I haven't started it. Let's talk about that in science class, all right? Assuming the Unificationists are the saboteurs, why do you think they're hiding equipment?"

"No one knows how they're breaking the lights," said Ivan. "But we've set up microdar sweeps, and we know they aren't just swimming up and breaking them with a hammer."

"I could have told you that," said Imina. "The cracks don't spread from a central point of impact."

Ivan glared at her. "So they must be using some sort of equipment," he continued, "to break the lights from a distance. The likeliest place for that equipment to be is somewhere in the habitat."

"Then why did you want to know if I'd found chemicals in the crates?"

"Because someone might be treating the glass with chemicals to weaken it. They're testing for that and other things in the labs right now. But if we found—"

"Search complete," the computer announced.

"Twenty-seven hits. Twenty-five are in the personal files of Nathalie Simeonov. One is in the personal files of Shahid Amadi. One is in the personal files of Marian M'Barra."

Color rose in Ivan Simeonov's face. "Computer, show me the reference in Mr. Amadi's file." He turned to Imina. She'd backed away and was standing in the center of the room. She knew she should be ready to run if he moved toward her, but she felt no urgency. She felt silly.

Ivan took a deep breath. "My mother *was* a Unificationist," he said steadily. "Many years ago. She left the party as soon as it started to become violent. She divorced my father when he wouldn't leave them. She is not a Unificationist now. Mr. M'Barra and the personnel directors of Living Planet know about it."

"Then why didn't you tell me?"

"Because I was afraid that if you knew, you'd believe she's the saboteur. And I'm even more afraid of what might happen if other people in the habitat find out. Now that people know the saboteur exists . . . Well, feelings are beginning to run high. If it isn't stopped . . ." The color faded out of his face. He looked grim.

Imina came back to the terminal. "So that's why you're looking for saboteurs. That's how you knew their slogans."

Mr. Amadi had used "the brotherhood of man" in a letter to a friend. He'd been describing how well people from all over the world got along in the habitat.

Mrs. M'Barra had used the phrase about "the needs of the many" in a note about an elective class in old movies.

"Nothing," Ivan muttered. "Damn."

"Could I try something?"

"You have an idea about the Unificationists?"

"No, this is something else," said Imina. "Computer, go into the thesaurus and get all the words related to magic—true magic—that aren't in common use, and search all files except reference, library, and news for them."

"Working."

"Magic?" Ivan's eyebrows almost touched his hair.

"Tell me, how are you doing with *my* science project?"

Ivan stared at her for a moment, then shrugged. "Pretty well, actually, though I'm not doing whale intelligence. They really aren't—"

"My grandmother's brother was a whale hunter," Imina told him. "And he saw some things. Once, they'd wounded a whale, and two others came to help it. One of them broke the harpoon shaft off, and then they carried the wounded one below the surface between them. What does that tell you?"

Ivan sighed. "I won't debate it with you. I admit I almost got sidetracked by the so-called whale language. Their calls are unique to each pod, and they sing a great deal. I think if you rigged a receiver to record the whole sonic spectrum and ran it through the right computer program, you might isolate thousands of distinct calls."

"But that isn't a language," Imina protested.

"Exactly," said Ivan. "That's why I decided to work on refining a microdar system for tracking undersea creatures, instead. I'm trying to make it sensitive enough to tell the different species apart by their shape, but so far—"

"What makes you so sure whales don't have a language?" Imina demanded. "Grandma Ata said—"

"Was your grandmother a statistics expert? We know whales aren't speaking a language, because if they were, we'd have translated it by now. Around 2020, lots of people did some very sophisticated work on so-called whale language. They did the statistics up, down, and sideways, and it lacked at least three-quarters of the variation that would be needed for a real—"

"You can't tell about a language using math." Imina glared at him. "You need a linguist. Someone who understands communication and how words gain meaning."

"Statistics isn't math; it's the reckoning of probabilities, using mathematical techni-"

"Search complete," the computer announced. "Three hundred and eight hits in the personal files of Annis Campbell. Forty-one hits in the psychology records."

"You're interested in magic, aren't you?" Ivan asked.

Imina ignored him. "Computer, what files in the psych records have those hits? Show them to me."

"We have no listing of psych records. Please clarify."

"*Uminukfa,*" muttered Imina.

"What?"

"It's Inuit swearing."

"We have no records of *uminukfa.*"

"Psychology records," Imina snapped.

"Thank you. Working. All hits are in the psychology records of Annis Campbell."

I am convinced she is lying to me. The phrase on the screen caught Imina's attention, and her scruples about prying fled. *But if she truly believes she is a shaman, she's going to have problems when that belief comes up against the reality that magic doesn't work. Especially since her belief in magic is inextricably linked with her love for her great-grandmother.*

"I never fooled her at all," Imina breathed.

It is primarily her belief that she is a shaman that separates her from other people, for she feels, probably rightly, that they wouldn't understand. This is particularly true of her mother, whom she blames for not understanding, since she is of the "same blood."

Imina flushed. "How could she guess? She'd make a good shaman herself."

All of this is made far more complicated by the unfortunate events that followed her grandmother's—

"Did they really confine you for psychiatric observation when your grandmother died?" asked Ivan.

Imina had forgotten he was there. She slammed down a key that cleared the screen and turned to glare at him.

He was gazing thoughtfully at her.

"Yes," she said. "I was working a spell with Grandma Ata when she died, and when they found me . . . I was upset. I talked too much."

"So you think you're a witch?"

"A shaman," Imina corrected him. "And I'm not the only one. There are other people making magic in the habitat. They're who I'm looking for."

"Then permit me to suggest you might be behind the times in your terminology," said Ivan. "Computer, search all files for terms related to parapsychic activities."

"Working."

"You mean like ESP?" asked Imina. "That's not the same as magic."

"How do you know?"

"Because I know about magic," Imina told him. "My grandmother was the last living Inuit shaman. And she was teaching me. I've seen magic work. I've done it myself, and I know."

"They could," said Ivan, "just be different words for the same thing."

"No," said Imina. "Psychic power comes from inside you. When you do magic . . . well, some of it's psychic, but most of it comes from the spirits and from inuas, the spirit that every living thing possesses. That's how come I could talk to the mice."

"The mice? The ones you let go in class? You think that was magic? You really are crazy."

"You can think what you want about that," Imina said, "as long as you keep it to yourself."

"But—"

"If you don't," she continued over his protest, "I'll tell everyone your mother was a Unificationist."

"Search complete," the computer interrupted the brooding silence. "One hundred and ninety-six hits. One hundred and seventy-three in the personal files of Dr. Ricardo Sandoval. Fifteen hits in the psychology files of Mr. Darru M'Barra. Eight hits in the psychology file of Dr. Ricardo Sandoval."

"Computer, show me the hits in Mr. M'Barra's psychology file." But Imina didn't watch the screen. "Ivan, I . . . I won't tell about your mother, if you don't tell about me."

His expression relaxed slowly. "All right," he said. "I guess everyone has secrets. Speaking of which," he gestured to the terminal, "should we be doing this?"

Imina remembered her father's lecture on privacy and blushed. "You didn't care about that when it was you looking for Unificationists," she told him.

They both looked at the screen.

Ivan whistled. "His psych rating is practically off the chart!"

"That explains it," said Imina. "'He frequently answers questions before people ask them, especially when he isn't concentrating, although he tries to suppress this tendency because he knows it makes people uncomfortable.'"

"'And he often senses what they're feeling.'" Ivan read on. "That must be useful for an administrator."

"But it takes him off my list," said Imina. "Good. I didn't want it to be him. Computer, let me see Dr. Sandoval's psych—psychology file.'"

"Not near as high a rating," Ivan observed.

"But higher than most people's." Imina read on. "So he became . . . a debunker?"

"He exposes psychic frauds," said Ivan. "It's his hobby. Mostly he finds flaws in the statistical methods people use, but sometimes he exposes out-and-out con men. He talks about it sometimes. Didn't you know?"

Imina shook her head. "I've only been here a couple of months. But that would be a good cover for someone who makes magic, to expose frauds and pretend to be a skeptic. Computer, let me see the hits in Dr. Sandoval's personal files."

"Annis, I don't—"

"Access denied! Access denied!" the computer told them. "You have violated security procedures." Ivan raced for the door. "The room is sealed. Please wait here. Security personnel will arrive and release you shortly. Access from this terminal is closed off."

Ivan slammed his palm onto the touchplate. The door didn't even twitch. He tried again. "Damn!" He whirled to Imina, who had frozen by the terminal. "We're locked in."

"You said this couldn't happen! You said your program was safe!"

"It must have tripped something else. Security's been notified."

"Do we have security in the habitat?"

"Not really. It's probably whoever's in charge of maintenance." His face was white. "If they catch me here, they'll think I was working for my mother."

"Then they won't catch you," said Imina impulsively. "Help me haul this crate off the big floor hatch. Hurry!"

Ivan shot to help her. "Thank you!" he whispered as he opened the hatch and lowered himself in. "I can't thank you e—my God, there's something down here! It looks like—"

"Get your head down," Imina snapped. "They might get here any second."

Ivan crouched obediently. "But what are you going to say when they find you here?"

"I'll think of something," said Imina, closing the hatch over his head. She was still thinking when the maintenance men opened the sealed door.

CHAPTER 5

"ALL THEIR LIGHTS HAVE BEEN DESTROYED," *said the Singer. "And they are still here."*

"Perhaps . . . perhaps we should wait," said the Young-one. "It took time for them to come. Perhaps it will take time for them to go."

"Perhaps," said the Singer, "they have no intention of going, and are using this time to decide how best to find us and retaliate."

"We don't know that," the Young-one objected.

The Eldest stirred. "Breaking their lights has not rid us of them. It is time for harsher measures."

～～～～～～

Imina was grounded. She glared furiously at the

locked door of her room, wishing she knew what her parents were saying on the other side.

They had been wholly baffled by this latest stunt. Her mother had cried when the maintenance men brought her in. Her father was angry, but willing to listen. Unfortunately, Imina still hadn't thought of anything to say, so she refused to answer their questions. But that didn't mean they had the right to lock her up! Well, two could play at that game. She sprang to her feet and flipped the switch that locked the door from *her* side. Immediately the room felt less like a prison and more like a sanctuary.

She flung herself down on the bed. Sanctuary was better than prison, but both left her alone. She couldn't think of any other ways to find the magic makers. It would have been nice to impress them with her cleverness, but it hadn't worked, and every attempt got her into more trouble. It was time simply to call them and ask for their help.

Imina pulled down the blinds so Stupid wouldn't interrupt her. Then she turned off her intercom in case her parents had a change of heart and wanted to yell at her some more. Finally, she settled cross-legged, with her amulet around her neck and Grandma Ata's shaman belt at her feet.

"*Aja-ja,*" she began to chant softly. "*Aja—*"

Beep! Imina jumped and gazed around wildly.

Beep! It was her computer terminal. Imina rose

and went over to it. The message signal was flashing. But it had never beeped at her before.

"Computer on. What's the message?"

Annis? Is that you? the words scrawled swiftly across the screen.

"Uh, yes," said Imina blankly. She'd never received a message like this before.

This is Ivan, the words continued to scroll. *I commed you, but your intercom's off, and I was afraid—*

"How are you doing that?" asked Imina. "I've never seen this before. Are you reading what I say now?"

Of course. That's what voice transmit mode does, though it isn't used much. I have to talk to you. The—

"You can't talk to me," said Imina. "I'm grounded."

Will you listen to me for a minute? This is important! The hatch you shoved me into had a narrow beam transmitter in it. It's set to track a specific satellite and is operable only if you have the proper codes. There's no reason anyone in the habitat would have something like that unless they had to transmit something in secret! It must belong to the Unificationist! It's proof!

"Why weren't there any marks in the dust around it?"

The transmission paused. *I suppose he doesn't use it much.*

"As in, never? Ivan, this only tells you that there is

a saboteur. What you need to know is who."

I realize that. We have to find some way to make the saboteur use the transmitter. Then we can watch the room and see who comes.

"You can watch. I'm grounded."

I'm sorry about that. But it won't be forever.

"How do you know?"

I need your help. How can we make the saboteur go to the transmitter?

"Send him a message saying you know who he is and you'll keep silent if he gives you a million Swiss standard," snapped Imina. "Ivan, I really don't care—"

But who do I send the message to?

"Send it to everyone. I don't care. I'm in too much trouble as it is, and I'm going to bed. Computer off."

Imina waited for a moment after the screen died, but the terminal remained dark. She gritted her teeth. It was his fault she was in trouble, the techy twit. Well, she didn't need him. She would find the magic makers herself.

"Aja-ja. Aja-ja." It took a while to get her anger with Ivan and her parents out of the way, but the trance was easier to find this time, as if making the decision had lowered some barrier in her will.

Brothers in magic, sisters in spirit.

Listen, I beg you, heed my call.

I need you, brothers and sisters of my soul.

I need your knowledge, I need your wisdom,

I need you, I need you, I need. Her mind was open. Her heart was open. The core of inner light that was her power flowed strong as a spring river along the paths where her song sent it. Then it died. She felt it die, like a flame when a soaked blanket is thrown over it. She tried again. And again. But even sending with all her power, she couldn't push the song past the blanket of silence. Something was blocking her spell.

Either she was a total failure as a shaman, or the magic makers were refusing her. She felt no sense of their presence. Maybe there were no magic makers. Maybe she had imagined hearing their spell down in the bottom of engineering. Maybe Dr. Kent was right, and there was no magic, and she was crazy.

She opened her eyes. Her grandmother's spirit stood before her.

Imina's mouth opened, but nothing came out.

The spirit sat down, cross-legged, and stared at her with her grandmother's wise black eyes, crinkled at the corners. "You look thin, child. Are you eating all right?"

"Grandma!" Imina tried to grasp her grandmother's shoulder, but her hand passed right through it. She gasped, then reached out and passed her hand through the spirit again. She felt nothing, not cold, nor warmth, nor energy. Nothing.

"If I'm the first spirit you've summoned, you

haven't been practicing enough, Imina." Her grandmother's voice was stern, but her eyes sparkled. If Imina looked hard, she could see the opposite wall of her room through the spirit's body. She stopped looking hard.

"Oh, Grandma." Two tears ran down her face.

"Huh," the spirit snorted. "That tells me absolutely nothing. If you want my help, you'll have to talk to me. I'm no more a mind reader now than I ever was."

The familiar sharpness made Imina laugh through her tears. "Oh,—"

"Grandma," the spirit finished for her. "I'm glad to see you, too, and I've missed you, too, and I love you, too. But you won't be able to keep me here indefinitely, so tell me the problem."

Imina did, letting the whole story tumble out.

Grandma Ata listened as she always had, without interruption, nodding occasionally. When Imina finished, her grandmother was frowning. "I've told you before, the spirits will call you when you're ready, and not a bit sooner. Have a little patience. As to finding these . . . what did you call them? Magic makers? I can't help you much. You do need more training in magic. Not as much as you think, but some. And they wouldn't be blocking your call if they wanted to train you. Even if you find them, you may still have to learn magic on your own. You'd best be ready for that."

"But Grandma, I don't *want* to be alone."

"Then don't be," said her grandmother. "Your real problem is that you're trying to fight the world, instead of living in harmony with it. That never works. You have to be in harmony to accomplish anything, especially magic."

"But this world has no place for magic! Grandma Ata, what's the use? There are no tribes to need a shaman anymore. They've all been taken from us." The tears welled again. "Everything has been taken from us."

"Huh. White people can't take anything that you don't want to give them, child. It's time you understood that."

"What about a tribe? What about a purpose?"

"You want a tribe, find a tribe. Build a tribe. As for purpose . . ." This time it was the spirit who reached out. Her hand passed through Imina's knee, and she grimaced.

"I was thirty when my only child was born, and I knew I would never have another. He didn't have the power to be a shaman. I thought like you then. I thought, What's the use of magic anymore? And I went down to the edge of the water and threw my belt into the sea.

"Then my great-grandfather's spirit came to me. I heard his voice in the beating of the waves and the cry of the wind, and he told me there was still a need for magic in the world. That I must keep it alive and wait, for the day was coming when my power would be needed. And the waves washed my belt onto the beach at my feet.

"So I kept the knowledge of magic alive. I changed the spells to keep them in harmony with a changing world, and I learned to work them in English when the old language died and I knew no child would grow up with Inupiaq as his heart's tongue. My son had a daughter, and she didn't have the power, either, and I was growing old. But I remembered my great-grandfather's words, and I waited.

"Then you were born, and I knew my waiting had been worthwhile. Your parents' jobs took them all through the world, so they gave you to me to raise."

Imina felt her power draining away. The image began to fade, but the voice was still strong. "I saw your power, even as a child, and I knew that one day the spirits would call you, and our magic would survive in you when I was gone."

The image vanished. The voice was going. "But then I was dying, and the day of need had not yet come . . ."

The voice faded out. The spirit was gone.

Imina rose to her feet and almost fell. She hadn't realized how exhausted she was. She crawled to her bed. She never remembered falling asleep.

~~~~~~~~~

"Annis?" Her mother sounded nervous, even through the intercom. "There's someone here who wants to see you."

Probably Dr. Kent, Imina thought sourly. She had slept late and awakened to the sound of knocking. At first she had thought it was Stupid, but the blinds were drawn. The knocking had been coming from the door. When she turned on the intercom, her father asked to come in. Grandma Ata's shaman belt lay in the center of the floor.

"No," she had yelped, scrambling to pick up the belt and conceal it.

"Suit yourself," said her father, and the intercom had clicked off.

She had put the belt and amulet away, then showered and dressed. It felt silly just to unlock the door and come out, but she was beginning to get hungry. Seeing Dr. Kent would be awkward, but at least it would give her an excuse to open the door. "All right," said Imina. She turned off the lock, and the door swished open.

"Hello, Annis," said Mr. M'Barra. "May I come in?"

He could read minds. Imina froze. Mr. M'Barra waited patiently. There was a tired crease between his brows, but he didn't seem angry.

"Uh, sure," said Imina, trying to keep her mind blank. If he could read her thoughts, he'd find out everything!

Mr. M'Barra took the chair at her desk. Imina perched on the edge of the bed, and he turned his chair to study her. He didn't look like he was picking knowledge out of her brain. A sliver of memory flickered through her mind. *He often picks up the surface thoughts of those around him, when he isn't concentrating on it. If he consciously tries, the ability is blocked.* He was concentrating on her now. He might be able to tell how she felt, but probably not what she thought. Well, then, keep him concentrating.

"Um, what can I do for you?" Imina asked.

"You can tell me where you got that access breaker program you were using," said Mr. M'Barra.

Straight to the point. Imina had expected a trap question. Honesty was almost impossible to evade.

"I'm sorry, Mr. M'Barra, but I *can't* tell you that. It doesn't have anything to do with the broken lights. At least, not with causing it. I swear."

He stared at her. Could he sense she was telling the truth? Mr. M'Barra rose abruptly and went to gaze out the window into the sea. There were no fish passing, but Imina knew he could see the colorful garden of animal life that filled all the areas touched by the lights.

"Annis, do you know why the habitat was built?"

She blinked. "To raise plankton. For the fish in the fish farms to eat."

"But man has never tried to grow plankton in the

past. Do you know why it's so important to do it now?"

"Well, because of the Unificationists. The crop virus."

"Go on."

"But you know all this."

"I want to know what you know. Go on."

"The Unificationists wanted to take over the world. So they created a virus to make all the food crops poisonous."

"Not poisonous. It works at the molecular level, so that the nutritive elements in the plant can't be absorbed into the bloodstream. But go on."

"So they turned up at the Council of Nations and said, 'Give us the world or we'll turn the virus loose' and . . . well, the governments tried to stall, and everyone was panicking, and somehow the virus got loose." She paused. He waited. "It's spreading gradually, so we don't have to panic, but we'll need to feed people from the sea. The fish people eat are at the top of the food chain. To increase the yield at the top, you have to increase the yield at the bottom as well, so Living Planet built the habitat. Lots of habitats, actually."

Mr. M'Barra waited, but she was finished.

"It isn't only Living Planet," he continued. "There are Matsashu Agronomic's water worlds, and at least a dozen political consortiums are involved in massive sea-farming projects. Because five years from now we'll be feeding the entire population of the world, more than nine billion people, almost entirely from the sea. And we'll have to go on feeding them that way for fifty years, before the cycle of the virus runs out."

"But the virus doesn't kill plants, it just makes it so people can't eat them. And not all plants are affected. There'll still be some fruit we can eat."

"All grains, nuts, vegetables, and about four-fifths of the fruit crops will be rendered inedible for almost fifty years," Mr. M'Barra told her. "If it affected grasses, all the animals on the planet would probably die. As it is, we'll have to struggle to preserve at least a third of the species. We'll probably lose most of the grain-eating birds. And we must do it without over-taxing the resources of the sea, because that would be fatal."

Imina gazed at his stiff shoulders. "I know," she whispered. "I'm sorry."

He shrugged and turned away from the window. "We can't do much about that. But have you thought about what would happen if, for any reason, the sea-farming projects failed?"

"But the plankton project's been working great."

"It isn't now," said Mr. M'Barra. "It's dark out there. We've kept the force nets up. One crop isn't that important, and they tell me it's worthwhile to see what lives, and for how long, when the lights go out. But nothing more will grow down here until we have light again. And it's no use setting out more lights until we find out what's breaking them."

"I truly don't know that. And neither does the person who gave me the program."

Mr. M'Barra was watching her. "What would happen if the habitat failed?"

"We . . . we'd have to move."

"What would happen if all the habitats failed?"

"We'd . . ." Imina's stomach knotted. "But that won't happen. I mean—"

"It's dark out there right now." Mr. M'Barra gestured to the window. "And we don't know why. Or how. Or who. What makes you think it can't happen again?"

"But surely we'd find some way to stop the virus."

"That was the first thing they tried. They tried very hard, and they came to the conclusion that it can't be done."

"Then . . . we'd all starve."

"Not all of us." Mr. M'Barra turned back to the window again. "Some people have already stockpiled food. There'd still be some fish in the sea, no matter how badly we depleted it. We could kill all the species we can't domesticate. Maybe twenty percent of the population could survive. The strongest and most ruthless twenty percent."

"You mean they'd fight. You mean war."

"I mean a kind of war we've never seen in all our history. Not only nation against nation, but neighbor against neighbor. I mean two people trying to kill each other over a handful of fish." He faced her squarely.

"I believe you when you say that to the best of your knowledge, the program you ran had nothing to do with the sabotage. But there may be things involved that you don't know about. So I have to know everything, even if it seems irrelevant. Where did you get the program?" He waited. Imina felt cold. He'd trapped her after all, in the strongest net there was. He'd trapped her with the truth.

"I'll tell you tomorrow," she said. "You're right, you have to know. But I owe it to my friend to talk to him first."

Mr. M'Barra hesitated, then nodded. "That seems fair. But don't wait too long. I can't see any reason for it, but I have a feeling I need to hurry with this."

"You think something else is going to happen? But the habitat is shut down. Even if there are saboteurs, what else would they do? And why? Why would anyone want to sabotage the habitat?"

"Not all the Unificationists were caught. Their leaders escaped."

"But even the Unificationists shouldn't want to sabotage the habitat. If everybody dies, there won't be any world left to take over."

"The Unificationists claim to have a cure for the virus. We don't think it's true, but if they can stop the plankton projects, or even make people believe they can, they might end up ruling the world after all."

"But if they don't have a cure for the virus, they'd have to put the habitats back. They'd have to be crazy."

"Most people," Mr. M'Barra rose, "are quite certain that the Unificationists are crazy. Think about—"

"Paging Mr. M'Barra. Paging Mr. M'Barra." The voice on the intercom was urgent.

Mr. M'Barra pressed the button. "I'm here, Chad."

"We need you in the clinic—now. It's Wu Tran." The voice paused painfully. "He's dead."

"On my way." Mr. M'Barra was gone almost before he finished speaking.

Imina thought. About Ivan, who had an illegal computer program and an ex-Unificationist mother, but who had been searching, just as she had. She was sure of that. Almost. She jumped to her feet and hurried after Mr. M'Barra.

She had to tell him everything. Maybe Ivan wasn't a Unificationist, but he might know something without knowing it, as he'd thought she might. She only hoped the Unificationists proved less elusive than the magic makers.

There was a crowd by the open access when Imina slipped into the clinic. They were gathered around a body that lay sprawled on the floor with water pooling around it. Imina could see only the slack, skinsuited legs. She looked away.

Ivan stood at the edge of the group, and Imina joined him. "What are you doing here?" she whispered.

"Shh."

"I'll have to do an autopsy, of course," said Dr. Pennyfeather grimly. "But it looks like suffocation."

"It can't be!" a man wearing a wet skin suit protested. "The first thing I did when I saw him floating was to check his mask, and it was working!"

"Tell it from the beginning," said Mr. M'Barra.

"Tran and I—" The man swallowed. "We'd gone out to examine the lights. We wanted to be sure the fracture pattern on all of them was similar, and we were going to bring more of them in for testing. We started at the far end of the north quadrant. Tran went down the line one way, and I went the other. We were in sonocom communication, so there was no reason not to separate."

"I know. Go on."

"We were at opposite ends of the line when I heard something. At least, I thought I did. A kind of whining, but very thin—distant. I tried to call Tran, but the sonocom sort of hummed off-key for a

102

moment and went dead. I tried again, but I couldn't raise him. So I swam back to where we'd left the skid and took that down the line looking for him, because the skid lights are so much stronger than a belt light, you know? I found him at the end of the line. He'd snapped his belt to one of the lights, as if he were going to work on it, but when I found him, he was just floating there. It couldn't have been more than ten minutes since the sonocom went. I checked his mask and it was working, but I couldn't take chances, so I popped one of the skid's emergency masks over his face and tried to resuscitate him. But nothing worked." His voice grew rough. "So I brought him in."

"You did everything right," said Mr. M'Barra. "You did all you could."

"That doesn't help Tran much, does it?" the man said bitterly.

Dr. Pennyfeather took the dead man's mask and strapped it over his own face. He dunked his head into the open access and stayed there. It looked ridiculous. No one even smiled. He waited for several minutes, then surfaced.

"Nothing." His voice was muffled. "Try the sonocom in the other mask."

The diver held the mask over his face. "Testing."

"I hear you," said Dr. Pennyfeather.

The diver dropped the mask. "But the sonocom

wasn't working! I swear it wasn't. This is absurd. Those things can't just break and unbreak. They've been tested!"

"Take it easy." Dr. Pennyfeather gripped his shoulder. "We believe you."

"I know." The diver rubbed his face. "But this is a nightmare. It's like black magic."

Imina's hand clamped around Ivan's arm. Elusive magic makers. Elusive saboteurs. Machines broken, no one able to tell how.

"What is it?" Ivan whispered, prying her fingers off his arm.

"Ivan, we have to get that mask."

CHAPTER 6

"AND STILL, THEY ARE NOT LEAVING," *said the Singer. "I was right, and have been right all along. We must attack the warm-ice-reef itself."*

The Eldest considered the rest of the quorum. The Singer throbbed with power and anger, but the Young-one . . . Working the death spells had left her shocked and torn by regrets. As for himself . . . "We will need more power for such an attack," he said. "It will take time for other Makers to hear us and come."

"We might," said the Singer, "be able to get all the power we need from them. I have an idea."

~~~~~~~~~~

"Are you insane?" Ivan demanded. "They have to run

tests on that mask. We couldn't get it for days."

"That would be too late." Imina glanced around the corridor outside the clinic. No one else had come out, but she lowered her voice anyway. "The more time passes, and the more people handle it, the less I'll be able to tell about the spells that were worked on it."

"Spells? As in magic? You think your so-called *magic makers* killed Mr. Wu?" His voice was rising. Imina pulled him down the corridor.

"Our best bet would be to get it from wherever they take it for testing. Where will they take it?"

"How should I know? You're the one whose father is chief engineer. Probably the big repair bay where they work on the skids. It has the most equipment. And how, pray, do you plan to get the mask out of there? And what on earth do you plan to do with it?"

"I'll go into a trance and try to see what spells were cast on it. Maybe I can even tell who cast them. And you can chant for me and lend me some power. I'm afraid I'm going to need it."

"Chant for you?" Ivan came to a stop. "Chant what, for God's sake?" He was staring at her.

Imina grabbed his arm and tried to pull him along. He didn't budge. She sighed. "You just chant *Aja-ja, aja-ja,* over and over. It will help me go into a trance, and it would summon good spirits to help me. If

106

they were speaking to me, that is."

"Spirits? You mean ghosts?"

"Mostly," said Imina. "But not entirely. Do you mind not having this conversation in the hallway?"

Ivan looked around as if he'd had no idea of their surroundings, then took her arm and marched off. "And where," he murmured, "is all of this going to take place?"

"In the bottom of the maintenance sphere," Imina told him. They passed into a section of living quarters. "I've found a good place for spells. It's connected to the earth. Where are we going?"

"My room." Ivan turned abruptly through a door, pulling Imina after him. They passed through the living room without pause, and Ivan didn't release her until the door of his room swished shut behind them. It was cluttered with the crystal and fine wires of electronic equipment.

"Let me get this straight. You want me to help you steal a mask that may be an important clue to the sabotage, and then go down to the bottom of the maintenance sphere and *chant* over it?"

Imina met his eyes squarely. "Yes."

"Then you are crazy."

"Maybe. But you owe me. If I hadn't covered for you yesterday, the whole habitat would know about your mother by now. I didn't even tell Mr. M'Barra about you—though I promised him I would tomorrow. We have to tell him what we know, Ivan. It might be important."

"I know." Ivan paced between heaps of disassembled equipment. "I just wanted to have something solid before I went to him."

"Then now's your chance. Help me get that mask, Ivan, and maybe we will be able to learn something."

"I'd like to examine it," he admitted. "But there's nothing I can do that the engineers won't. Trying to get the saboteur to use the transmitter is a better idea. If I had his codes, *I* could handle the transmitter. But they probably won't be in the database. It's not secure enough."

"You couldn't prove it by me. What happened to your security-proof program, anyway?"

"It was a new system Mr. M'Barra added recently. It trips the alarm when an abnormal number of files are accessed from any terminal."

"And you couldn't get around that?"

"I could have if I'd known about it. I'll have to, if I'm going to search the database for the transmitter codes. But I don't think they'll be there."

"Then the mask is your best bet. If we can find out who tampered with it, you can search his rooms for the codes. Can't you check everything on the mask as well as the engineers can?"

Ivan nodded.

"Then you wouldn't be hurting the investigation

by taking it. As soon as I'm finished, you can examine it, and if you find something, you can go straight to Mr. M'Barra. And if *I'm* right, it won't matter how long engineering has that mask. It will be in perfect working order."

"All right," said Ivan. "I'll help you."

"You will?"

"I owe you for covering for me—I don't want anyone to connect my mother to this. And if I can find something wrong with the mask myself, maybe it will help Mr. M'Barra. But after this, we're even."

"Fine." Imina's heart lifted. She hadn't realized how much she'd wanted Ivan's help until he'd offered it. "How do we get the mask?"

"Get your diving gear," said Ivan. "I have an idea."

"Um. Hi, Dad. This is Ivan."

"Hi, honey, Ivan." He didn't look up.

Imina's skin suit dripped on the floor of the big repair bay. She and Ivan both carried their masks. It looked perfectly natural. She hadn't expected it to be her father who was working on the mask. At least he hadn't taken it apart yet. She looked up and met Ivan's eyes. *Distract him*, he mouthed.

"Uh, Dad? I'm sorry about Mr. Wu. He was on your staff, wasn't he?"

This time her father did look up, but his hands stayed on the mask. "Hell of a way to get out of being grounded, huh?" His voice was full of grief. Imina winced.

"I'm sorry, honey." Her father turned to face her. "That was a rotten thing to say. I feel rotten, that's all."

"It's all right, Dad. I just wanted to tell you I'm sorry about last night."

She hugged him, and he twisted in his chair and hugged her back, hard. Imina's eyes were wet when she pulled away. Ivan nodded once behind her father's back and swung the mask that dangled from his fingers. He must have succeeded in making the switch.

"I'll see you tonight." Her father turned back to the mask on the workbench. "Nice meeting you, Ivan."

"Thanks, Mr. Campbell." Ivan took Imina's arm and pulled her away.

"I hated that," said Imina, as she climbed down the ladders to the bottom of the sphere. "I was using him. I didn't expect it to be Dad."

"It's a good thing it was," Ivan told her. "You wouldn't have distracted anyone else that easily. And you were the one who wanted the mask."

"I know." Imina bit her lip and pushed regret aside. "Come on. We're here." She led the way over the slippery sloping floor until she was settled in the center.

110

Ivan crouched beside her. "What do you want me to do?"

"Give me the mask." Imina took it from him. "Now, just chant the way I told you. *Aja-ja, aja-ja.* That rhythm. And while you chant, think about helping me. No, *will* to help me. Then I can use your energy."

"I thought you wanted to summon spirits to help you."

"It would be better if you were dead," said Imina. "But I'll take what I can get. Now chant."

"Is that the source of magic power? Spirits, living or dead?"

"There is no source of magic power—it just is. Like the rocks and the sea. Like gravity. And everything has it. Even technocrats. Now chant."

"*Aja-ja,*" said Ivan dubiously. The glow from their belt lights was eerie on his face. "*Aja-ja.*" It took several minutes for him to settle into a rhythm, but once he did, it formed a counterpoint to the machinery above it. Imina began timing her heartbeat against the two rhythms, and soon her mind sank through the darkness into light.

With the mask in her lap, holding her palms just above its surface, not quite touching, she could feel the lingering remnants of the spell. It prickled her palms, like the itch of a bad sunburn. Disharmony. Off-center. Off-key. Wrongness. This was the spell.

Deeper now, deeper. The mind, the will behind the casting. Presence. Many minds. Anger. Fear. Determination. Sorrow. The memory of their minds in the remnants of the spell that still lingered on the mask. They didn't feel familiar. At all. Strange. Alien.

Go deeper. Another presence. Very faint. Fear. Then panic. Can't breathe. Terror—

A jarring blow snapped Imina's head around. She gasped. A second hard slap connected with her cheek.

"Stop." Struggling upward through the layers of the trance, another blow rocked her. "Ivan, stop." She reached out and grabbed his hand. "What did you do that for?"

"You appeared to be distressed." Ivan looked rather anxious himself. His intent gaze searched her face. "You were having trouble breathing. In fact, you weren't breathing. You were turning blue."

"I'm sorry. Thanks." Imina clutched his hand. "I found Mr. Wu's death. He was killed by magic. They stopped the motors on the mask. They threw it into disharmony, and it stopped, and he couldn't breathe, and he died."

She was crying. Ivan freed his hands and pulled a tissue out of one of the sealed pockets on his belt.

"Thanks." Imina blew her nose. "Ivan, what are we going to do? It's the magic makers who are sabotaging the habitat. We ought to tell Mr. M'Barra, but he won't believe us. And they have to be stopped!"

"First," said Ivan, "calm down. I have to examine the mask. If I can find—"

The clang of a hatch above them wasn't loud, but they both heard it. Feet sounded on the rungs of a ladder.

"They're only one level above us," Ivan breathed in her ear. "How do we get out of here?"

"We can't," Imina whispered. "Not without passing them." The footsteps had reached the floor over their heads.

"Nope." The woman's voice came clearly from above them. "Even this relay is working fine."

"Then where the hell did that power surge come from?" A man's voice, ringing with frustration.

"I don't know," said the woman. "But it wasn't us. All our equipment is working perfectly."

"Then why is the whole north sector of force nets blown to hell? There has to be something wrong with the equipment. There's no one down here but us."

"Are you sure about that? The Unificationist leaders all escaped, you know."

"So you think one of them just moved in and is sabotaging the habitat? That's crazy, Lola. They're the most wanted men on the planet."

"Well, how do you explain it? It has to be sabotage. Sooner or later we're going to find out who, and then—"

"Then what? You plan to take the law into your own hands? I've heard people talking about that, and it scares me a lot more than these so-called Unificationists."

"Would you rather let the habitat be destroyed piece by piece? Who do you think it is, if not Unificationists?"

"Maybe some nut." The footsteps rang on the ladder again. "Somebody went aquaphobic and just flipped out. It's more likely than a Unificationist conspiracy."

"Without anyone noticing? Come on . . ."

The voices faded.

"They've taken out the force nets," Imina murmured. "But why? The habitat is already shut down."

"Come on." Ivan tugged at her arm. "I want to get a look at this mask. We have to put a stop to this, fast." He scuttled quietly for the ladder as he spoke.

"You won't find anything," Imina told him. "They stopped it with magic. And I don't understand why they'd do that, either."

"All I know is that soon this entire station is going to be hunting Unificationists," said Ivan grimly. "And I know who they're going to find. I just hope the saboteur put his codes into the computer. He's probably got it written in a damn notebook, stashed somewhere I'll never be able to find."

Imina stopped. "Ivan, what kind of notebook?"

"How should I know?"

"No, I mean, what would the codes look like?"

"It could be anything from math to poetry. But there should be quite a few pages of it. Why?"

Imina was frowning. "Dr. Sandoval had a notebook in his desk. It was the only hard copy he had. I thought it looked like some sort of puzzle, but I wondered why he doesn't keep it in the computer with everything else."

"It's flimsy," said Ivan thoughtfully, "but it's worth a try. I can send the blackmail note to his terminal in the classroom tomorrow morning."

"The blackmail note? Ivan, that was a joke."

"It's not a bad idea."

"It's a terrible idea. Besides, Dr. Sandoval's a technocrat! He couldn't be a magic maker."

"I'm looking for Unificationists, not shamans."

"You should be looking for shamans," Imina told him. "God, I'll never be able to convince *anyone* of that. They'll think I'm crazy. They'll lock me up."

They had reached the open access that led out of maintenance. Ivan opened an equipment locker and pulled out one of the spare masks. He put it on and was about to dive when Imina caught his shoulder. "Ivan, you believe me, don't you? About the magic makers?"

"I believe you believe it. I'm going to take a look at this mask. You can come, too, if you want." He plunged into the water and vanished.

"Well, thanks a lot," said Imina to the empty room. She went to the locker and found a hood and a pair of gloves that fit. Let him examine the stupid mask all he wanted. He wouldn't find anything. The magic makers had destroyed the north sector of force nets. Maybe she could find something there. Imina tugged on her mask and slipped through the access into the sea.

Stupid caught up with her before she swam halfway around the sphere. Usually, he irritated her, but today she caressed him as he bumped against her, strangely comforted by his presence.

She circled until she reached the northern edge of the habitat, then found the cable that serviced one of the lines of magneto-poles and started to swim along it. When she left the ring of light that flowed from the habitat, she turned on her belt light, adjusting it downward so she could see the thick cable, half-covered with silt.

When the first of the magneto-poles appeared, she stopped to examine it, but she couldn't see anything wrong, except that it wasn't producing a force field. Oh well, what did she know about the machines? Maybe the engineers could figure out what caused the power surge.

Clinging to one of the struts, Imina looked back at the habitat. It rose erratically from the sea floor, a haphazard mound of glowing bubbles—a ridiculous structure. It must be the darkness surrounding it that made her think of it as a fortress of light. She never had before. Before this, she hadn't realized how much she'd come to care about the place. She had once thought of it as a jail.

Imina turned and swam on. Her belt light illuminated the sea floor and cable. Between the places where life had gathered around the broken lights, she could see current ripples in the mud of the ocean floor. The same sluggish current pushed her sideways as she swam, stealing a little of her strength.

As she approached the fourth magneto-pole, the ripples on the bottom changed. Imina frowned and swam down to look more closely. A set of ridges around the magneto-pole went at right angles to those caused by the prevailing current. They were smaller than the ripples the current built, covering a rough circle several yards wide. A faint haziness of disturbed mud blurred the area—the current was erasing them, even as she watched.

The next magneto-pole was near one of the shattered lights. She could see no disturbance in the sea life around it, so she swam on. The magneto-pole after that was surrounded by bare mud, and again she saw the odd ripples, marching against the current. Something had swept the sea floor around the magneto-poles, going across the direction of the current. The mysterious power surge the maintenance people had talked about? Imina swam on.

At the next pole, the ripples were undisturbed. Or were they? Imina looked closely, and it seemed that the ripples surrounding this pole were smaller than the ones around them, as if the power surge, or whatever it was, had changed directions and moved against the ocean current. Was that possible? It certainly seemed odd. Imina made up her mind and swam away from the cable that fed this line of magneto-poles, following the track of the mysterious force.

Her light hit the cable that linked the next line of poles only a few minutes after she thought it should, but she had to cast down the cable for some time before she found the next pole. Yes. The strange force had passed through this pole, too, and again it had made ripples that opposed the ones around them.

For more than an hour Imina followed the mysterious track, sometimes across the current, sometimes against it, always away from the habitat. Shoals of small fish darted around her, drawn by her belt light, but only Stupid stayed.

Even for a person accustomed to diving, it was a long swim. She stopped to rest several times, knowing she needed to reserve enough energy to return. Rest would have been easier if she hadn't been so excited. She was following the tracks of power, and she knew of only one thing that could have pulled it so wildly out of its natural course.

Two-thirds of the way through the sector, she began to notice an odd discoloration on the magneto-poles, as if the metal had been heated. Then the poles became bent. Then warped. The next few poles she passed looked as though they'd exploded. Then one, so twisted it almost doubled over, but whole. Imina turned back.

After twenty minutes of circling, she thought she'd found the place the power had come to. She was between two of the poles, and the current pushed her. She knew she should tie her belt cord to the cable beneath her, but the thought of Mr. Wu's body tethered to the broken light made her shiver. The water seemed to resonate with memories just beyond her perception. Could she hold herself against the current and still go into a trance? No. Imina swam down, dug beneath the cable and passed her belt rope under it. She floated up when she was finished, watching the current carry the mud she'd disturbed into the surrounding darkness.

She swept her light around for Stupid. The last thing she needed was him nudging her out of a trance. But for the first time today, he was nowhere to be seen. Maybe he was smarter than she thought.

She relaxed in the water and took a deep breath. "*Aja-ja aja-ja.*" The soft, constant hum of the motor on her mask had no rhythm, unlike the big machines in maintenance. It wouldn't help her. Imina abandoned the chant. If it took a deep trance, she could always try again. She concentrated on relaxed, deep breaths. In and out. In. Out.

The images swarmed into her mind as soon as her barriers lowered, as if they were eager to reach her.

A shaman had died here. Swollen with pride, power, and anger, a shaman had died. He had tried to pull power directly from the force nets, and the power had come, filled, and destroyed him.

Imina shook her head, shaking off the light trance. Now that she knew, she could sense the anger and pain without it. Something about the emotions made her think of the spell that had stopped her call. Had this magic maker been her enemy? If so, it didn't matter. He was dead.

Her stomach was churning, and inside a full-face diving mask was not a good place to be sick.

She swam down and freed her rope from the cable. She had to use her wrist compass to orient herself, but once she was sure of the direction, she swam straight for the habitat.

A maker of magic had died. All she had to do was discover which of her suspects was missing, and she would know, really know, who one of them was. Who one of them had been.

CHAPTER 7

THE SINGER'S DEATH SILENCED ALL THEIR PROTESTS, *even the Young-one's.*

"We need more power for the final attack," said the Eldest. "But we will get it from a source we understand. It is time to summon the others to our aid."

⁓⁓⁓⁓⁓

Stupid rejoined her during the long swim back. Imina was glad to see him, but she didn't stop until she thrust her head out of the open access in the clinic and saw Dr. Pennyfeather hunched over his worktable.

"It wasn't you," she whispered. "Thank God." She propped her elbows on the rim, took off her mask, and rubbed her stinging eyes.

"Here now. What's this?" Strong hands pulled her from the water. She tried to stand, but her knees were rubbery. "Goodness, m'dear, you're exhausted. You've been out much too long. That water is cold. Even a thermal skin suit can only do so much." He rubbed her back and legs.

"I'm all right," said Imina shakily. "I just wanted to be sure you were . . . here."

"Ah. Any numbness? Tingling anywhere?"

"No." She shook her head. "I didn't change depth at all. I promise. I'm not decompression sick, just tired."

"And chilled," said the doctor. "Allow me, m'dear, the gentleman's privilege of walking you home."

"But I'm fine." She should check on the others. "Really. I can get home on my own."

"Of course you can." The doctor released her shoulders and her legs buckled. He grabbed her. "But a lady should encourage chivalry. How will we learn to be knights, if the damsels won't at least pretend to need rescuing?"

He chattered all the way back to her family's quarters. Imina's legs grew steadier as they walked, but she was too glad he was alive to try to shake off his company. A warm shower took the last bit of tension out of her muscles, and she barely had the energy to eat before falling into bed. The next thing she knew, her mother was waking her to get ready for school.

Mrs. M'Barra was in the classroom when she got there, and the mice were back in their cage. Was Dr. Sandoval the magic maker?

Lisette was insufferably smug. She kept looking at Imina and dropping remarks about Mouseketeers, whatever they were. The mice bothered Imina. Why hadn't the evil eye worked? They should have avoided those traps as long as her power sustained the spell. Was she so poor a shaman—

Dr. Sandoval came into the room, and Imina's breath caught. That meant Mr. M'Barra had to be the one who was missing. Mrs. M'Barra was reading to the little kids. She didn't look like her husband was missing. And Dr. Sandoval didn't look like a Unificationist spy.

Was Ivan going to go through with the plan he'd talked about? If he was, she'd better make sure everything looked normal. With a stab of nervousness, Imina turned on her terminal. Dr. Sandoval didn't appear to notice anything unusual, and she realized that she often didn't start work until he arrived. She glanced at the others. Lisette, Daud, and Reba chattered, ignoring the math lesson on their screens. Dr. Sandoval started them working on his way to his desk. Ivan appeared completely absorbed in calculation.

Dr. Sandoval sat down before he noticed the message flag. He murmured a command to the computer, completely at ease. There were often messages on the terminal in the morning. Then his eyes widened. Imina, watching from under her lashes, saw all the muscles along his jaw leap into prominence as he read. She realized she had no idea what Ivan had told him.

He punched the button that extruded the keyboard and began to type furiously. He would be trying to find the source of the message, but Imina trusted Ivan to cover his tracks. Dr. Sandoval's mouth was tight, but he had looked the same when he found Imina in his rooms and thought she was playing a trick on him. It didn't prove a thing.

She sent a message to Ivan's terminal, and he scowled, typed back one word, *later*, and closed her out. It wasn't until lunch that she succeeded in talking to him.

"Of course it doesn't prove anything." Ivan spoke so softly that Imina had to lean forward to hear him. They had found a vacant table, but there were people all around them. "It won't be proved until he goes to the transmitter."

"Even if he does, what will you do? It'll just be our word to Mr. M'Barra against his."

"I talked to Mr. M'Barra about the mask," said Ivan.

"When?" Imina interrupted. "When did you talk to him?"

"After I examined it." Ivan looked surprised at her vehemence.

So it wasn't Mr. M'Barra who'd died. Then who was it? None of her suspects were missing. Could it be one of the people she'd dismissed? Someone who'd faked their answer to her scrying question? Mrs. Bouchard was standing a few tables away, talking to some friends, so it couldn't be her.

"I took it to his office and told him what we'd done," Ivan went on.

"You told him about the magic?" Imina's voice rose. "What did he say? Did he believe you?"

Ivan grimaced. "About the access breaker program and the mask," he said. "Magic and shamans are your problem. I was in enough trouble as it was."

Imina winced. "Was he mad?"

"Yes," said Ivan. "That's why we have to catch Dr. Sandoval with the transmitter. Guilty knowledge, they call it. So I sent him the note."

"What did it say?"

"Just what you suggested." Ivan's voice dropped lower. "That I knew he was the Unificationist who was sab—"

"But I was joking! I didn't mean for you to do it."

"It was a good idea," Ivan insisted. "I told him I wanted the money in gold, not credit. He'll have to go to the Unificationist leaders for gold, and that means he'll have to use the transmitter, so we'll—"

"The Mouseketeer and the technocrat. Aren't they cute?" It was Lisette's voice. She and Reba sat down at a nearby table where they could listen to everything Ivan and Imina said. Imina glared at them, then turned to Ivan, who was scowling, too.

"How do you know he's not doing that now?" she asked, trying to phrase it so Lisette wouldn't understand.

"Because he's eating lunch," said Ivan. "I'm going there as soon as school's over. Will you meet me?"

"They have a date," Lisette whispered loudly to Reba.

Ivan picked up his tray, pretending to ignore them. "Meet me there." He walked away.

Lisette and Reba giggled.

On her way out of the cafeteria, Imina took a quick detour into the closet where the cleaning supplies were stored. It took several minutes to find the mousetraps, their glowing red beams shut down, now that they'd done their work. She picked one up, reaching out with a shaman's senses. She felt no trace of the spell she'd cast. Even if she'd done it wrong, some remnant of her magic should have lingered. No, this was *their* doing. Anger flared through her. She didn't know what they'd done, or how, but those other magic makers had no right to tamper with her spells, or her habitat. She would find them, stop them before they did more damage, killed more people. She was mad now. She clung to her anger. It felt better than fear.

Imina sent messages to Ms. Balinski and Mr. Hoenstauffen during a history test and got prompt replies. So it wasn't them. She bit her lip, tried Dr. Kent's terminal, and got an automated message that the doctor was in conference and couldn't be disturbed—it made her stomach twist. Ivan had talked to Mr. M'Barra, so all the others were accounted for. She'd been so certain Dr. Kent didn't believe in magic, but now . . . Was Dr. Kent the magic maker who cast the silence spell against her? Dr. Kent was an enemy, but not that kind of enemy. She *liked* Dr. Kent, even if she did think Imina was crazy. But Dr. Kent always made it easy for people to reach her.

"Annis? If you get stuck on one question, just go on. The test's not that important."

That was good, because Imina flunked it.

Mrs. M'Barra stopped her on her way out of the classroom.

"I'm sorry about the test," Imina said. "I just—"

"This isn't about the test." It wasn't like Mrs. M'Barra to interrupt. "I told you it wasn't important. This is. I'm worried about you, Annis."

"Me? Why?" Imina's mind raced. What could Mrs. M'Barra have learned? And how? It took her a moment to realize the teacher was blushing.

"All right." Mrs. M'Barra pulled her over to a corner. "Remember that I feel strongly enough about this to tell you, because this is a secret I don't want to get out. But if anything happened, and I hadn't warned you . . ."

Imina stared.

Mrs. M'Barra took a deep breath. "Annis, I cast your horoscope."

Imina almost laughed. Her face must have showed it.

"It isn't funny." Mrs. M'Barra shook her arm. "You're looking at some hard choices, there's a lot of danger, and I'm worried for you."

Imina sobered. Who was she to laugh at someone else's magic? "What can you tell me?"

"Not much that's useful," said Mrs. M'Barra ruefully. "You've been going through a hard time lately. Well, you know that. But it's coming to a climax—a handful of crucial decisions that will change the rest of your life, with consequences so far-reaching I couldn't begin to chart them."

"But what decisions? How should I make them?"

"I don't know." Mrs. M'Barra shook her head. "Too many variables. But the results of your choice . . . it was incredible! The possible consequences are virtually limitless. And lots of them are disastrous. Not only for you, either. It . . . it looks bad."

"If I make the wrong decisions, you mean."

Mrs. M'Barra nodded. "But I need to tell you, whatever decisions you make, you'll lose something. That was clear. All the possible paths involve danger and loss."

A chill whispered through Imina's heart. "I'll be careful. I promise." Then curiosity stirred. "Why is it a secret? That you're an astrologer, I mean?"

Mrs. M'Barra blushed again. "You may think this is silly. I suppose it is, but look at the people down here. They're all scientists! They'd laugh themselves sick. I wouldn't mind so much if it was just me, but there's my husband. He says he wouldn't be embarrassed, but . . ."

"I won't tell anyone," said Imina. "I understand better than you think."

Imina was pacing up and down the hall in front of the room that held the transmitter when Ivan arrived.

"What kept you?" she hissed. "He could come anytime. He doesn't have to wait for the dead of night, you know."

"I know." Ivan pulled her into a room down the hall from the transmitter. "Door open," he told the computer. "Lights off. Keep your voice down. I had to get rid of Lisette. She was following me." He sounded indignant.

Imina giggled. "She thinks we're having a tryst."

Ivan looked harassed. "Forget about her. I don't know when Dr. Sandoval will come. It could be in the dead of night, for all we know. I've set up a computer program that will trap him in the room, with the transmitter, but it will take a few minutes to activate. I need you to—"

"How does it work?" Imina interrupted. "We don't want him to catch us—if he comes at all, which I'm beginning to doubt. Ivan, he's our science teacher! How can he possibly be a Unificationist spy? The saboteurs are magic makers, and I can't believe Dr. Sandoval's one of them. He debunks psychics using statistics! He can't believe in magic."

"You believe in magic, but you don't believe in Unificationists? Don't answer that. I haven't got time to argue with you. I need you to go down the hall to room 152. Hide yourself so you can see the corridor, but someone looking from a lighted corridor into a dark room can't see you. As soon as I have my program ready, I'll contact you through voice transmit mode. When you see Dr. Sandoval, go into the room with the transmitter, press the X key, and I'll activate the program. It will tell the computer that multiple files are being accessed from the same terminal we were using the other night. You saw how that worked. If he stays there just a few minutes—"

The dark room encouraged quiet. Ivan's voice had risen to a murmur, but it wasn't loud. Imina reached out and clamped her hand around his arm. In the sudden silence they both heard the footsteps coming down the corridor.

Ivan dove for the door and then stopped, realizing that the swish might be heard in the hall. Imina pressed her hands over her mouth as the footsteps came closer. It might have been anyone coming to get something out of one of the stored crates, but she knew it wasn't. A door swished open and then closed.

Ivan leaped for the panel that concealed the computer, yanked it open, and began to fumble behind the terminal. "God, I didn't think he'd come till night," he muttered, as strings of test characters raced across the screen.

"Ivan, the dust." Imina's heart pounded. "He'll see the marks in the dust and he'll know—"

"No, he won't." Ivan's face was set. "I programmed the maintenance machines to clean the empty quarters last night."

"Connection functional." The computer's voice sounded terribly loud. "Computer on."

Ivan's fingers were flying over the keyboard before the computer stopped speaking. It probably took less than two minutes for him to implement his program. But to Imina, listening for the swish of a door opening in the corridor, it seemed much longer. Ivan stopped typing. The cursor blinked. Imina's pulse drummed in her head.

"Access denied!" the computer said loudly. "Access denied! You have violated security procedures. The room is sealed. Please wait here. Security personnel will arrive and release you shortly. Access from this terminal is closed off."

The door remained open.

"We did it." Ivan sagged against the wall. Even in the dim light from the open door, she could see drops of sweat on his face. "He's trapped in there. When the maintenance people come we can tell them . . ." He swallowed. "We can tell them about it, and they'll get Mr. M'Barra. With the transmitter in there with him, and the code book in his room, he can't deny it. We've got him. It's over."

Dr. Sandoval had returned her physics test today. She'd gotten a seven. Imina was shaking. "I can't face this." She forced her wobbling knees to move. The corridor. Out of here, before the maintenance people came. Before all the questions. Before that door opened and Dr. Sandoval came out. She bumped into the door frame.

"Annis, are you all right?"

Imina shook her head and began to run.

She told her parents she had the flu, and they

believed her. She said she didn't want Dr. Pennyfeather, she just needed sleep, so they left her alone. She pulled up her covers. Her hands and feet were cold.

Dr. Sandoval was a spy. He must be, since he knew where the transmitter was. But he wasn't a magic maker; Imina would bet on that. He couldn't have killed Mr. Wu.

If the magic makers were working for the Unificationists, maybe he'd know who they were. If he named his accomplices and one of them was missing . . .

It was a long time before she slept.

Mrs. M'Barra, her face stiff with shock, announced that Dr. Sandoval had been arrested and that she'd be teaching all the classes for a while, so she'd need their cooperation.

There was no chance to talk to Ivan until lunchtime. He was sitting alone at an empty table. Imina didn't know how he'd found that much privacy in the crowded cafeteria, but she was grateful. He looked like he'd gotten even less sleep than she had.

"I'm sorry," she said as she set down her tray and slid into the seat next to him. "Running out on you last night was a rotten thing to do. I just . . . couldn't face him."

"I understand." Ivan pushed his tray away. He hadn't eaten much. "I don't blame you."

"Was it awful?"

Ivan nodded. "He'd smashed the transmitter. He was tearing up the code book when they went in. There isn't any doubt. In fact, Mr. M'Barra told me they were about to question him. There were discrepancies in his personnel file. His real father was a Unificationist leader, but his mother divorced him and remarried, so his last name changed. They got suspicious when they found so little about his real father in his file, so they called Dr. Kent to get her opinion on his psychological condition."

"Dr. Kent? When was this?"

"Most of yesterday. A careful study of his psych records showed they'd been tampered with, so they would have caught him anyway. We just gave them proof."

"Then Dr. Kent was here yesterday?"

"Working with Mr. M'Barra most of the day, I think. I saw her last night. Why?"

"Because that means she isn't the magic maker."

Imina told him everything. When she finished he shook his head. "But Annis, none of your suspects is missing."

"A magic maker died. I'm sure of that. Did Dr. Sandoval name his accomplices?"

"Yes." Ivan's voice was bitter.

"Who were they?"

"He said he had only one accomplice in the habitat, Nathalie Simeonov. And no, she is not missing."

"I didn't ask that. I never suspected your mother."

"They do." He gestured at the crowd, and Imina realized that most of the people near them had turned their backs on Ivan, or were watching him surreptitiously. This was why he had the table to himself.

"I'm sorry," she said. "But Ivan, why would he lie?"

"Then you think my mother's a spy?"

"Don't be silly. Your mother couldn't possibly be a magic maker, she's too techy."

"She is not!" Ivan took a deep breath, and his whole body slumped as anger left him. "I'm sorry," he muttered. "It's just that, damn it, it's not fair! My mother left that stupid party when it started to get violent. She gave the police a lot of information that helped them stop the Unificationists in the end, and that hurt her. And now Dr. Sandoval has gotten revenge for that, and it's hurting her again."

"Then let's find out who is doing it," said Imina. "Ivan, this is our first real clue. A magic maker died yesterday. It may not be one of the people I originally suspected, but someone is missing from the habitat. If we can find out who, we'll know who one of them was. All we have to do is get a complete personnel list."

"You can't do that. Mr. M'Barra classified all the personnel files. Access is no longer open."

"Can't you get around that?"

"I probably could, but I don't know why I should."

"Because we have to have a complete personnel list to figure out who's missing."

"I had to give all the copies of my access breaker program to Mr. M'Barra."

Imina just stared at him.

"All right," he sighed. "But if there isn't anyone missing, will that convince you there are no magic makers?"

"If we do find someone missing, will that convince you that there are? Ivan, we have to do this. We must!"

He sighed again. "I was going to spend the afternoon working on my microdar. I got some information from Dr. Pennyfeather on whale bioneurology, and I've got the microdar adjusted so it will detect only whales. Of course, adjusting it so it will differentiate between the species will be harder, but I think I can—"

"How long will it take you to write a new access breaker?" Imina interrupted.

"Probably all afternoon," said Ivan reluctantly.

"Come to my room after dinner and I should be ready for you."

"'And shouted but once more aloud, / My father must I stay' . . . um, I forget what comes next," Marinka admitted.

"'While o'er him fast through sail and shroud, / The wreathing fires made way.'" Imina looked at the clock again. Literature would be over in twenty minutes, and she'd be free to go.

The little kids weren't really taking centuries to learn their verses of the silly poem, it just felt that way. Imina knew it by heart, and if she had to sit through it one more time, she'd scream, or hit a kid, or do something awful.

"Mei-lin's turn," Mrs. M'Barra prompted gently.

"'They wrapt the ship in splendor wild,' um, um." She turned hopefully to Imina.

Imina sighed. "'They caught . . .'"

"'They caught the flag on high, / And streamed above the gallant child, / Like banners—'"

The call twisted through the bones of her skull and set them vibrating. She couldn't quite make out the words, but she knew what they meant.

They summoned her. They summoned Makers of Magic. They summoned her.

The call faded, leaving an ache behind her eyes.

"Annis?" Mrs. M'Barra was staring at her.

"It's nothing," said Imina. "Look, I have to go. I, uh, I have a headache."

"I'll take you to the clinic." Mrs. M'Barra was beginning to sound alarmed.

The call came again, even clearer. Its purity and power rang in her bones. She could barely see Mrs. M'Barra's face, but she forced a smile and managed to say, "No, I'll go myself. But I must go. I must go now."

She hurried out of the room. She had no memory of walking through the halls, but when the call ceased, she was only two doors from her quarters. Where her skin suit was.

The call came again as she was fastening her mask. When it stopped, she found herself in the open ocean. The water around her was dark; she could see only a few feet. She turned on her belt light, looked at the depth gauge on her wrist, and was relieved to discover she was close enough to the bottom that she didn't need to worry about decompression sickness. Even so, she swam down till the sea floor was within reach of her light.

Without the call, she wasn't sure what direction to swim in, so she waited. Somehow she knew that the reason the call started and stopped was to give distant magic makers a chance to get a bearing on the location. It would come twice more. She had only to wait for it.

Then the summoning came, and she answered, swimming blindly toward the call.

A hand closed on her ankle, pulling her back.

She shook it off and went on swimming. The hands reached farther and grabbed her belt. Then they closed around her wrists, stopping her forward motion, and she struggled until the call ceased.

The other diver was Ivan, and he was glaring at her. Imina stopped fighting and waited until he released her wrists. He tapped the side of his mask, and she reached up and turned on her sonocom.

"Are you out of your mind? What the devil do you think you're doing?"

"I was answering the summons," she told him.

"What summons? Whose summons? I didn't hear any summons!"

"Of course not. You're not a shaman."

Ivan grabbed her shoulders and tried to shake her, but the water blunted the force. He held on to her, taking deep breaths. "You mean you received a summons from those people? And you're going? Just like that?"

"Not me in particular," said Imina. "They're summoning all magic makers within range of the call."

"Hasn't it occurred to you that it might be a trap? They might be summoning you to your death!"

Imina felt as if someone had punched her in the stomach. "But they . . . No . . . You can't . . ."

Her conscious mind shuddered awake. "My God, they're powerful," she whispered. "They were reeling me in like a yo-yo. I didn't think at all. I just went. I never *dreamed* a summoning spell could be that strong. Especially against a shaman, who actually hears it."

Ivan took a deep breath. He looked as if he wanted to start asking questions, but he suppressed them. "Let's get back to the habitat, shall we?"

Imina flashed her light around. Nothing but the sea floor and dark water. "My God, I didn't even notice the direction. I don't know where the habitat is!"

"I do," Ivan told her. "Come on."

Imina braced herself for the final call. Since she was prepared to resist, it didn't compel her, but swimming in the opposite direction was like swimming through mud. She was glad Ivan kept looking back to be sure she stayed with him.

Ivan's coverall was too big for Imina, but she rolled up the sleeves and cuffs and wore it anyway. They'd gone straight to his room to shed their skin suits. They had too much to discuss to wait for Imina to get her clothes.

"So that's what happened," she finished. "I didn't even think about what I was doing until you grabbed me. How did you know I was in trouble?"

"I didn't. Mrs. M'Barra sent me to be sure you got to the clinic. She was worried about you."

"I'm grateful to her. If you hadn't stopped me, I'd have swum right out into the ocean."

"All you had to do was activate the homing arrow on your compass," Ivan pointed out. "Or set off the emergency signal. Someone would have grabbed a skid and come straight to you."

Imina shivered. Then she thought of something. "Was the emergency signal on Mr. Wu's mask on?"

"No," said Ivan. "I hadn't thought about that. Maybe he panicked and didn't think of it. It wouldn't have saved him; no one was closer to him than the diver who brought him in, and he got there as fast as he could."

"But if the motor on his mask was off when he pushed the button, the signal wouldn't come on, would it?"

"That mask was in perfect working order," said Ivan. "I checked it completely, twice."

"Then why is Mr. Wu dead?"

Ivan rose, went to his terminal, and began to type.

"What are you doing?"

"Writing a new access breaker program. You might as well go get your clothes. This will take a while."

So Imina went home and changed. She stopped to tell her mother she'd probably have dinner with a friend, and not to expect her home till evening. Her mother was delighted she was finally making friends.

It was almost dinnertime. Imina stopped at the cafeteria and picked up a couple of sandwiches for Ivan and herself. Then she found Ivan's mother, told her she needed Ivan's help with her science project, and asked whether they could eat in his room. Mrs. Simeonov, who looked strained and tense, simply nodded. Imina felt sorry for her, but there was nothing she could do except what she was doing.

"I've got sandwiches," she told Ivan triumphantly as she entered his room. "And I fixed it with our parents. We can eat here and go on working."

"Fine," Ivan muttered. "I've almost got it."

Imina put his sandwich on a stand by the bed, and started eating her own as she looked over his book cartridges. Nothing but techy stuff. She grimaced. The most interesting thing in his room was a wide screen with glowing green dots on it. Some were moving, the others were still. "What's this?"

"My microdar," he told her absently. "Don't touch it."

"You mean those dots are whales?"

"Um."

"That's great. How many are there?"

"Only a few. They've been hanging around the habitat. In fact, one of them was caught in the power surge the other day and killed. The engineers found the body. A humpback."

"Really."

"Got it!" Ivan spun the chair to face her. He started to speak, but the sandwich caught his eye and he went to get it before returning to his chair. "A' right," he mumbled, his mouth full. "What files d'you want?"

"First, a complete personnel list for the habitat."

Ivan swallowed and made the request in the clear precise tones he used to the computer.

"List complete," the computer told them.

Ivan's mouth was full again.

"Can you make a list of all the people who've used a computer terminal in the habitat in the last twenty-four hours?" Imina asked it.

"Yes."

"Then do it, and subtract everyone on that list from the complete personnel list."

"Working . . . Ready."

A new list flashed on the screen. Thirty-four names were left. Imina's parents had mentioned a few of them, but she didn't know them. She looked at Ivan. He shrugged.

"How are you going to find out if they're missing?"

Imina thought a moment. "It's dinnertime. Computer, list the comm numbers for those people's quarters." She commed their rooms and asked to speak to them. When they answered, she closed the connection. Only six weren't there. She paged them over the intercom. Two answered from workstations. Four were in the cafeteria. The last one wanted to know who this was, and what was going on. Imina cut him off. She was sweating with tension and embarrassment. "Everyone is here."

"I told you it wouldn't work."

"But someone has to be missing. A magic maker died!"

"Look, I'm not wholly convinced about magic. But you did seem to be following something today, and you were swimming away from the habitat, out to sea."

"You mean," Imina struggled with the idea. "You mean the magic makers have their own undersea base? Outside the habitat?"

"A vehicle, more likely," said Ivan. "Why not? The Unificationist leaders could afford one. It would be easier to do the sabotage that way than from within the habitat, and it would also explain why the investigation inside the habitat keeps going nowhere."

"And," said Imina, "they could have their own magic makers working for them. No wonder I can't feel a familiar presence in the spells."

Ivan shrugged. "All they'd have to do is park their

craft outside the range of the habitat's sensors. They could use skids to move in any equipment they need. If anyone saw them, they'd think they were from the habitat. Except maybe Mr. Wu saw something suspicious."

"You're right," said Imina with growing conviction. "They must be outside the habitat. That would explain everything. But will Mr. M'Barra believe this? It sounds pretty far-fetched."

"He was really angry about our taking the mask," said Ivan. "He absolutely forbade us to do any more investigating on our own."

"Then we have to have proof before we tell him," said Imina.

Ivan nodded. "I'll get us a skid. One with decent sensors. Tomorrow after school we'll follow the line you were swimming on and see what we find."

CHAPTER 8

"WE CAN SILENCE THE IDIOT-SONGS THAT SUS-TAIN THEM," *said the Eldest. He felt the attention of twenty-one Makers like a pulse over his skin. They were all here, the Elders, the Young-ones, the Mothers, the Far-seers, the Weather-shapers, the Singers, the Healers, even the Ghost-speakers.* "We can turn their lights into darkness. We can destroy them. How say ye, Makers, peace or war?"

"War." The word eddied around the circle, gaining power as it passed. There was no dissent.

"To the death," the Eldest finished.

~~~~~~~~~~

For the first time since she'd come to the habitat, Imina did a spot check on her diving gear. Ivan was making the same checks. You were always supposed to do it, but no one bothered. The equipment always worked.

She had been anticipating this moment all day. School had been horrible, the clock alternately creeping or racing, depending on whether she was feeling impatient or terrified.

"Let's go," said Ivan.

They put on their masks and swam to the maintenance bay where Ivan had requisitioned a skid. It was parked outside the sphere, waiting for them. Her father had once described the skids as "instrument panels with legs," though the long tubes of the propulsion system didn't resemble legs at all. They reminded Imina of sleds, the old-fashioned kind that reindeer or horses used to pull, with the top open to the sky, or in this case, the sea. The skids were habitat property, and minors weren't supposed to use them without adult supervision. When Imina asked Ivan how he'd gotten it, he said, "Called in a favor. I can handle routine maintenance on these things as well as anyone. Sometimes that's useful."

Under his directions, Imina helped check the skid even more thoroughly than they'd checked their masks. Engine. Thruster pumps. Lights. Emergency air supply. Ivan checked the sensors himself. Minors weren't supposed to be given skids with the delicate sensor apparatus at all.

"You must have been very useful," Imina said aloud.

Ivan shrugged. "I want you to watch the sensor panel," he told her. "I'm setting it to show anything with more than five pounds of metal in it. The radius on a skid sensor is only half a mile, so if we find them, we'll be close. It probably won't do much good to look for anything inside the range of the habitat's sensors, but I'll leave them on to give you some practice interpreting the screen."

"What's the range of the habitat's sensors?"

"About three and a half miles." He misinterpreted Imina's widened eyes. "I know that's not much, but when the facility was built, no one thought we'd need cyclo-yipe!"

"Stupid!" Imina pushed the big fish away.

"Friend of yours?" Ivan was grinning.

"He follows me all the time." Imina glared at the grouper. "I can't get rid of him—except when I found the place the magic maker died and could have used some company. Then he left."

"He wasn't with you when I found you yesterday, either. Maybe you're losing your charm."

"How far are we going?" Imina demanded, ignoring Stupid's friendly bumps.

Ivan eyed the grouper thoughtfully. "The fuel cell has enough power to take us about twenty-five miles. I thought we'd go ten miles past the edge of the habitat's sensors, with the edge of our sensors touching the line you were swimming on. If we come back along the same line, on the other side, we can cover an area ten miles long and two miles wide, and still have some power left if we need to go out of our way to investigate something."

"How much power left?"

"Not a lot," Ivan admitted. "But if we find anything, all we're going to do is identify it and come back and tell Mr. M'Barra. So we don't need a lot."

Imina nodded. "Is there a photog unit on this skid?"

"Yes. I've checked to be sure it's working."

"How long will this take? If we're not going to be back till midnight, I'd better tell my parents something."

"With the pumps on high, it should take less than three hours. That's one of the reasons we needed a skid."

"Then let's go," said Imina.

The thrumming of the pumps, sucking water into the front of the skid and expelling it out the back, was loud even underwater. They were moving faster than Imina had ever taken a skid, but they still couldn't outdistance Stupid, who seemed fascinated by the skid's big lights.

Near the buildings of the habitat, the sensor showed a solid sheet of brilliant green.

"It's set pretty high," Ivan explained. "And we're surrounded by machinery. Wait till we clear the complex."

He was right. As they pulled away from the spheres, darkness, interrupted by dots of green light, washed slowly down from the top of the screen. The dots formed patterns.

"Which are the lights, and which are the magneto-poles?" Imina asked.

"The lights should be less bright," Ivan told her. "What it's actually picking up is concentrations of metal, and there's less of that in the lights."

The small blue dot that represented the skid was headed straight for one of the weaker green dots. As they approached it, the whole screen faded slowly to green. Gazing away from the brightness, Imina saw the shattered light as it passed a few feet to their left. She watched thoughtfully as the pattern on the screen faded back in.

"We're at the end of the habitat's sensor range now," Ivan told her. "You're familiar with the light and post pattern. If you see anything out of place, let me know."

"No, I was going to keep it to myself," said Imina. "Ivan, what if they put their equipment in the same spot as one of the broken lights? If they took the light away and dumped their own stuff in its place, we would never know."

Ivan thought about it. "Let's hope they aren't that smart."

Time passed. The light pattern of the plankton fields flowed off the sensor screen and was replaced by darkness.

"Would you like me to drive awhile?" Imina asked.

"No," said Ivan. "Just keep your eyes on the screen."

"But there's nothing on it. Why can't I drive?"

"Because I know where you were swimming, and you don't."

Imina went back to the sensors. More time passed. She was about to demand that Ivan give her the compass heading and the controls, or she was going to go play with Stupid, because he was better company than Ivan and the screen put together. She'd rehearsed this speech twice, and was just about to say it when a pale streak of green, translucent as a ghost, flickered on the sensors.

"Ivan, I think there's something here."

He came to look. "It's awfully faint. It looks like someone scattered a ton of bolts. It couldn't be a machine. It's not dense enough."

"Maybe they're magic bolts," said Imina. "Let's check it out."

Ivan eyed her dubiously.

"You admitted yourself, you have no idea how they did it." Imina gestured to the screen. "This is something else you don't understand. Maybe they're connected."

Ivan turned the skid. Stupid darted away and vanished in the dark water. Imina glared after him. Stupid fish.

The green wash on the screen grew brighter as they approached, but it was still transparent when the blue dot of the skid slipped over its edges. Imina looked down.

"Manganese nodules," said Ivan in disgust.

The sea floor within range of the skid's lights was littered with what looked like dirty, misshapen pool balls.

"What nodules?"

"Manganese. They're distilled out of sea water. They're not very dense. I'm surprised the sensors picked them up. I didn't think they were that sensitive."

"There must be thousands of them!"

"A mining company would be delighted," said Ivan. "I'm not. Come on. We're almost at the end of the outward sweep. We should cross over the line now and start back."

Something pricked at the edge of Imina's awareness. She flashed her light around. "Where's Stupid?"

"What?"

"Where's Stupid? He should be back by now. He never leaves me for more than a minute or two."

"That's not true. He wasn't with you yesterday at all. Our fuel is limited. We ought to . . ."

Ivan's voice went on, but Imina was no longer listening. Stupid had been missing yesterday when the magic makers worked their summoning spell. Stupid had vanished when she approached the place where the power of the dead magic maker lingered. Stupid was not here now.

Ivan was still talking.

Imina closed her eyes, sinking into herself like a seal diving to escape the harpoon. The sea around them was alive with magic. It teased her senses as she worked softly into the trance.

Ivan shook her shoulder, but she ignored him, stretching for the core of light within her. She touched it just as the sonocom moaned and fell silent. An odd, dissonant hum reached Imina's ears. Deep in the calm of the trance, she heard the motor on her mask struggling to maintain its own vibration against the off-key humming. It wavered and died, and the sound that stopped it was the only sound.

Imina took a deep breath and reached out with her mind. The spell pressed darkly against her. She exhaled and took another breath. There wasn't enough oxygen. Her lungs wanted more. The next breath would be worse. She held this one and tried to ignore the suffocating feeling as she grasped the power and shaped it into a ball. A great ball of light, of power, of will, her will, that no other power could penetrate. She moved the ball up and centered it on her head, and the motor on her mask hummed to life, clearing carbon dioxide out of the air she was breathing and replacing it with oxygen. Imina sucked in a deep breath, and then another, and the pressure in her lungs eased.

She looked around for Ivan. The skid had drifted to rest on the sea floor. With the lights out, she could barely see Ivan struggling with the panel over the emergency air masks. Even if he reached them, they wouldn't work. And his hands had begun to fumble already. Imina swam down and caught his shoulders, pulling her head close to his. She extended the shield to cover his head as well.

The sonocom crackled, and she heard his sobbing gasps. "God, God," he mumbled. "We have to get out of here. God." He lunged for the controls, and she had to stretch the shield to cover both of them. He was pressing touch pads, but nothing answered. He was distracting her. Imina turned her sonocom off. The faint hum of her mask was soothing.

She let the outer world fall away and contemplated her shield. It was strong and bright, fed by her will and her power. She pumped more energy into it and watched it grow, pushing the darkness of the death spell away from the skid.

The pumps shuddered to life. The skid heaved

beneath her, and she started to drift away, but Ivan grabbed her wrist, then tied something to her belt so the skid would pull her along. That was good. She couldn't maintain the shield spell and hold on to the skid at the same time.

They were moving, that was all she knew. Time was infinite and did not pass. Within the cocoon of the trance, there was only the sphere of her power and the pressure of the spell pushing against it. Eventually the dark spell started to waver. Then it vanished.

Imina didn't dare let her own spell go yet. She opened her eyes and saw the light pattern of the plankton fields on the sensor screen. Soon she saw the edge of the brilliant green wash that indicated the machinery of the habitat.

With a sigh, she let the shield fade.

Ivan had to drag her through the open access off maintenance. He took off his mask.

Imina fumbled with hers, and he reached out and tugged it over her head. "Ow."

"We've got them," he exulted. "Whatever stopped that skid has to have left some signs. It must have. No one has touched this skid but me, and no one's going to. I'll run every test ever invented until I find out how they killed those motors, and *how* will lead us to *who*. I know it."

Imina shook her head. "You won't find anything. It was magic. But it felt," she frowned, "*different* this time. Like there were more of them. Or maybe that was because it was aimed at me." She shivered. "If Stupid hadn't warned me, we'd be dead."

"Annis, maybe you should talk to Dr. Kent. She could probably help you."

"Not likely." Imina snorted. "She thinks I'm crazy."

Then the chilling realization came. "You think I'm crazy, too, don't you?"

"You seem to take it all so seriously," said Ivan. "Every time something happens, you twist it to fit your magic theory. We've both been frightened, and if you talk to Dr. Kent, you'll see how irrational your theory is."

"You bastard." Imina staggered to her feet and faced him. The spell had drained her. "I saved your life back there. By magic! You think I'm crazy? How do *you* explain what happened to the masks and the skid, technocrat?"

"Probably some sort of sonic disrupter." Ivan's voice was cold, but his cheeks were an angry red. "I thought I heard something just before everything went off. Then their equipment must have malfunctioned."

"Then I put up a shield," said Imina, "and held off the spell so we could escape. What do you think

I was doing in a trance all that time?"

"I know you fainted or something," Ivan told her. "It's all right. It was terrifying. *I* was terrified. No one could blame you for freezing. You don't have to rationalize it with magic."

Imina glared at him. "Damn you," she muttered. "Damn you to hell, you circuit-brained, techy twit."

Ivan's face was scarlet. "It's better than being crazy."

Imina turned and walked away.

She knew she was late for dinner and braced herself for her parents' reproaches. She was almost disappointed to find their quarters empty. There was a note on the terminal. They'd gone to an important meeting and might be late.

She made herself a meal and ate it, fuming. Thought he knew all the secrets of the universe, the closed-minded cretin. He'd be *dead* if it weren't for her!

But she needed to talk to someone. These magic makers were more than a half-trained shaman could cope with. She was going to need help—adult help. She grimaced. Not her parents. They were too wrapped up in her to pay attention to what she said. She needed an adult with an open mind. Someone who didn't think they knew everything already. Someone like Dr. Pennyfeather.

The lights outside the windows shone dimly into the

clinic lab. Dr. Pennyfeather was sitting at his work-bench, but he didn't appear to be working.

"Dr. Pennyfeather?"

He jumped and reached out to snap on one of the bench lamps. "Ah, Annis. Is something wrong, or are you just in search of companionship?" Lit from beneath, his craggy badger face should have been sinister, but he just looked older. He smiled, but Imina could tell it took an effort.

"You look like you need companionship," she said, coming into the room. "Is something wrong?"

"I asked you first. But since you look perfectly healthy and only naturally worried, I won't push it. Yes, I could use some companionship. I just came back from the meeting, you see."

"It's over? I'd better tell my parents where I am."

"Don't bother. Your parents are still at the auditorium, and the meeting shows every sign of lasting well into the night."

"But you left . . ." And came back to your lab to sit alone in the dark. "Dr. Pennyfeather, what's going on?"

He sighed. "Fear, mostly, but it's manifesting itself as hate. A common human reaction, but not a pretty one."

"But they caught the saboteur. He hasn't escaped, has he?"

"No, Dr. Sandoval is in decompression and will be

turned over to the authorities when the supply flight comes. Though with the storm blowing up, that may be a while."

"The storm?"

"It's hard to think about weather down here, isn't it? There's a storm coming in above us. No small craft in the air now, and if it gets worse, no large ones, which means we may have Dr. Sandoval with us for some time. I just wish he hadn't accused Nathalie of being his accomplice."

A chill chased down Imina's spine. "That's ridiculous. Dr. Sandoval—"

"Has not admitted to being the saboteur. He claims he did nothing for the Unificationists except gather information. He swears that he destroyed nothing and killed no one. He's very convincing."

"But no one could possibly believe Mrs. Simeonov is the saboteur. Nothing bad is going to happen, is it?"

"Oh no, I'm almost sure not. It's tricky, and I don't envy him, but Darru has the worst of the crowd well in hand, and I doubt he'll let them get out of it."

"Darru?"

"Mr. M'Barra. He has an excellent knack for controlling mobs. And he has many able supporters, your parents among them, so don't worry."

"Can't you help him?"

"Oh, I gave quite a fiery little speech about lynch

mobs, witch hunts, and evidence, but no one was paying much attention, so I left."

"They wouldn't really go on a witch hunt, would they?"

"Not if Darru has anything to say about the matter. But the will is there. And the man power. When people get like that, they start looking for scapegoats. Anyone would do, really, but Nathalie's background is unfortunate."

"What are they going to do to her?"

"Nothing, I hope. Darru was forced to place her 'under arrest,' and that seems to have placated most of them. Marian M'Barra took Nathalie back to the M'Barras' rooms with a full security force, so she'll be all right."

"What about Ivan? Was he with her?"

Dr. Pennyfeather frowned. "No, I don't believe he was. He'd be in his quarters?"

Imina went to the intercom and signaled the Simeonovs' rooms. "They aren't taking calls. Could he be in danger?"

"Not until the meeting ends, at least. Surely his mother sent for him. But maybe you should check his quarters. If he's there, get him out. We're probably being alarmists, but the mood of that meeting was ugly."

Two husky and slightly embarrassed maintenance

men stood guard outside the Simeonovs' quarters.

"He went in to pack some stuff," one of them told Imina. "But he hasn't come out. We're supposed to watch the door, so no one can 'tamper with the evidence.'" He grimaced. "They'd have a fit if they knew we'd let the kid in, but I'll be damned if I'm going to help harass them."

The other man looked uneasy, but he nodded.

Imina pressed the touchplate. The door didn't move. She tried again, but it still wouldn't open. It was the first locked door she'd encountered in the habitat. She pushed the comm button. "Ivan, it's me."

"The Simeonovs are not receiving calls," said the computer.

Imina looked at the guards.

"I don't blame him," said the first. "You want me to ask him to comm you?" The other guard shrugged.

Imina scowled. "Ivan!" she shouted. She pounded on the door with her fist. "Ivan, I have to talk to you. Open the door, damn it."

The door swished open. A soft chuckle from one of the guards followed her into the room, but Imina ignored it. Ivan's door was open. Like Dr. Pennyfeather, he was sitting in the dark. Unlike Dr. Pennyfeather, he was working.

"How can you possibly worry about that stupid microdar when your mother's just been arrested?"

"I'm recording the whale movements. They're bizarre. Every few seconds, one of them swims past the habitat from a different direction and—There one goes! Watch."

A green blip moved at an angle across the bottom corner of the screen, then stopped. A ring of similar blips gathered loosely around the edges of the screen.

"So what?"

"They aren't all in range," said Ivan. "I'd guess there are between twenty and thirty whales out there. My system for telling the species apart isn't completely functional, but I've gotten some readings, and I think some of those whales are of different species. There goes another one!" The green blip came from the other side of the screen, crossed a corner of the first one's track, and stopped.

"So what?" said Imina again.

"But whales always stay with their own species, with their own pod, in fact. As far as I know, a group of mixed-species whales has never gathered before. And they just swim past the habitat one at a time, in an arc from the bottom to the surface and down. And always at a different angle." He gestured at the screen where a third blip crossed the corner of the first one's line and was swimming out.

Imina frowned, drawn to the screen in spite of herself. "How come the picture gets fuzzy when they're at the top of the arc?"

"The storm is causing interference. There's a lot of lightning in it, and this equipment is sensitive."

"I still don't see how you can care about techy stuff when your mother has been arrested."

"I'm recording it," said Ivan. "Because we may never get a chance to observe this again. Not recording it won't help anyone."

Another blip moved, crossing the top corner of the second one's track.

"Have they decided what to do yet?" Ivan asked.

"About what?" said Imina absently.

"About my mother," snapped Ivan. "Are they going to call Living Planet's security, or try to handle it here? Are they going to charge her with the sabotage? Lock her up? Haul her down to the bottom of maintenance and pull off her fingernails?"

"I don't know," said Imina. "I'm sorry. Look, can you put all those lines on the screen at the same time?"

Ivan took a deep breath. "I suppose I could. Does it matter?"

"Please, I think it might." A fifth blip was swimming across the top corner of the screen. "Ivan, do it."

He sighed and went to the terminal where he extruded the keyboard and began punching keys. "Over here." He gestured to the computer screen. An intricate crisscross of lines appeared, centered on the habitat. Ivan frowned. "It's a geometric pattern. Though it's not quite precise. How odd."

"It doesn't have to be precise," Imina's voice shook, "as long as the lines connect. It's a web. A pattern to hold magical energies within a circle and intensify them."

"You recognize it?" Ivan's voice shot up. "That exact pattern?"

"Not quite." Imina shook her head. "The one my grandmother used was six-sided. This is . . . eight-sided?" As she watched, a glowing line began to track across the glass, connecting the last two ends. "Ivan, it's almost complete!"

"Let me get this straight," said Ivan. "You think the Unificationist magic makers have trained *whales* to work spells for them?"

The pattern was complete. The almost familiar sensation of the alien magic tugged at her awareness, but for once it was more important to think than to feel. She had to convince Ivan—now.

"They must have." She tried to speak calmly. "But," she scowled, "that doesn't make sense."

"At least you realize that," Ivan muttered.

"A web has to be shaped by the shaman himself. It's made of magic."

Imina gasped. No wonder the spells had felt so alien. No wonder they'd found no trace, in or out of the habitat.

"Are you trying to tell me," Ivan demanded, "that there are shamans out there *riding* those whales?"

"No," Imina cried. "How could I have been so blind? It's the whales themselves. The whales are making magic!"

Every light in the habitat went out.

CHAPTER 9

THE LIGHTS OF THE WARM-ICE-REEF ARE DARK. *Their idiot-songs are silent. In all the world nothing is heard but the song of the circle. They will die.*

⁓⁓⁓⁓⁓⁓

"What happened?" Imina stood still in the darkness. Her voice sounded high-pitched and squeaky. She cleared her throat and tried again. "Ivan, what's going on?"

"Power's off." His voice squeaked, too. "Hang on. I've got a hand light somewhere."

She heard him fumbling, the sounds sharp and high. Suddenly, she understood. The acoustic modifiers were off, so the helium in the atmosphere was distorting sounds. She started to giggle, but she was afraid of how weird it would sound. Then the implications hit her. "Ivan, it's not just the lights. The power's off!"

"That's what I said. Damn. I know I put that in here. No, I moved it." He groped his way around the room and began fumbling in a new place.

"How much air do we have?" Now that Imina's eyes were adapting, she could see the windows as lighter patches in the blackness surrounding them. She moved carefully to the nearest and looked out. She couldn't see a thing.

"About forty-eight hours," said Ivan finally. "At least in the upper levels. In the lower levels, it may start to go in a few hours, but the power will be restored long before that. What I don't understand is . . . gotcha!" A beam of light split the darkness, reflecting off the microdar and computer screens. In the dim backwash, Ivan's face was grim. "What I don't understand is what happened to the power in the first place."

"Maybe the surface generators went off?"

"All thirty-four of them? Those generators are separate units. You can't just flip a switch and shut them down. Something might have severed the power cables, but that would take an enormous amount of force, or an explosion. Surely we'd have heard it."

"Ivan." Imina's breath caught. "Could the water get in?" Aquaphobia whispered through her. She felt the tons of water on the other side of the wall as a pressure against her body, crushing the air from her lungs.

"No," said Ivan. "The open access ports work with atmospheric pressure, like holding an empty glass upside down in a tub. The few vents in maintenance that are held by force fields have an emergency back-up system that closes a door if the power goes off."

"But if the shaft to the surface was blown open . . ."

"I think we'd hear it if the habitat was flooding. And there'd be wind as the air was displaced. At least in the open areas." Ivan started toward the door, then stopped and swore.

"We can't get out." Imina's hands were clammy.

"Oh yes we can." Ivan went to his desk and pulled a long-shanked screwdriver out of the clutter. It was much stronger than the delicate ones used on elec-tronic panels.

"What do you use that for?"

"Prying things apart." He went back to the door, inserted the blade at an angle between the door and the jamb, and wrenched the door open. There was a slight dent in the thin metal panel, but once it was open, it slid aside easily.

"Come on. The outside door may be tougher, but my mom's got some tools that are stronger than this.

There's another hand light, too. I'll get it for you."

"Where are you going?" Imina followed Ivan into the main room. He lifted a floor hatch and began to rummage.

"To help get the emergency generator going. Or, if they get it on before I get there, which is likely, to help find the cause of the power shutdown."

"I don't think the emergency generator will work."

"Don't be silly. The emergency generator works on fuel cells, not power from the surface. There's a backup generator in case that doesn't work, and either could maintain essential life support for weeks. I can't think why the power isn't on already, unless . . ." His hands stilled. "Could the saboteurs have tampered with the emergency generators, too?"

"They don't have to," said Imina. "I don't think any machine will work inside the web. It's magic, Ivan."

He held up the glowing light. "This is a machine. Why doesn't your magic affect it?"

"Maybe . . . maybe because it doesn't make a noise. Remember the sound we heard when we were attacked on the skid? I think this spell works by disharmonizing machines that make a sound. Like the engine that runs the skid pumps. Like the motor that runs the pumps and filters on the diving masks."

"Disharmonizing?"

"I don't know how else to say it," cried Imina. "There's an Inupiaq word, but it has no translation."

Ivan rose from the floor and gave her a hand light and another heavy screwdriver. He jimmied the outer door open.

"Ivan." Imina caught his arm. "Ivan, you have to believe me. The whales are attacking the habitat with magic. If we waste all our time looking for mechanical causes, we'll die here when the air runs out."

He tried to pull away from her, and she tightened her grip. "You saw that pattern. You know how oddly the whales are behaving. Why won't you listen to me?"

"Because, Annis, the whole thing is simply too far-fetched. It's crazy. I went along with you because it served my own purposes, and because, well, I like you, nutty as you are, and I was willing to help out. I admit the whales' behavior is odd, and if I had to, I might admit that they might be intelligent. But magic? No. I'm sorry." He freed himself and hurried down the hall.

"*Uminukfa!*" Imina stamped her foot. It didn't accomplish anything, but it made her feel better.

She looked at the blank computer screen. Her proof was there, unless the power failure had wiped out the data. Could she shield a generator long enough to show someone? She took a deep breath and let her inner senses open. Even without a trance, she could feel the alien spell, rough and dense, scouring her nerves. She didn't have half the power needed to repel it. Which made perfect sense, since it was cast by a whole circle of magic makers. She was alone.

Desolation gripped her, but with it came the memory of Grandma Ata's acerbic voice, *You want a tribe? Find a tribe.* Imina blew her nose fiercely and went in search of Dr. Pennyfeather.

She stopped several times on the way to the clinic to free people who were pounding on their doors. One man was screaming. When she released him, he pushed her aside and ran down the hall. She heard him crash into something outside the range of her light and winced.

She stopped outside her family's rooms. She had to jimmy the door and the door of her bedroom, but the floor hatch opened easily. Her amulet: for courage, for cleverness, for love. It slipped softly under her collar. Her hands hovered over the shaman belt. Then she lifted it and hung it around her neck, too. It reached to her waist, bulkier than the amulet, but under her shirt, in the dark, no one would notice.

Dr. Pennyfeather was in the clinic. A surge of relief ran through Imina as she heard the soothing ramble of his voice and saw the wash of light from the clinic's open door.

Two men and a woman, holding hand lights, were

with him. Imina caught a glimpse of the mangled, blood-spattered foot they illuminated before she averted her eyes.

She started back into the hall, but the woman saw her. "Get in here, girl. We need more light."

With her eyes on her feet, Imina crept forward and gave them her hand light. Dr. Pennyfeather, intent on his work, continued his soft monologue without seeming to notice her. But who was he talking to?

A breathy moan answered her question. The man with the mangled foot was conscious. Her eyes flew to his face. It was gray and sweating, both contorted and oddly slack. He was drugged, but the pain was reaching through it. His hand clenched and then opened, groping.

Imina clasped and held it, even when his grip hurt. She tried to add her voice to Dr. Pennyfeather's, to speak soothingly to him, but her throat was too tight.

Her grandmother had taught her several healing spells, but Imina knew she would never be able to work them. She couldn't even look at the mangled flesh, much less touch it, work magic on it. No wonder the spirits never chose her. She was too cowardly to be a shaman. Why hadn't Grandma Ata seen it?

"There. All finished." The man's hand was slack. Dr. Pennyfeather reached down and lifted hers away. His hand was covered with blood. Imina shuddered.

"Sorry, m'dear."

The others lifted the injured man and carried him out.

"You did very well." Dr. Pennyfeather went to wash his hands. He didn't turn on the tap, just rinsed them in a layer of water in the bottom of the sink. With the power out, there was no running water. "Many people would have fainted at a sight like that." He picked up a bottle and gestured for Imina to take it. "Squirt, please." He held his hands over the sink. Imina upended the bottle and squeezed, and the sharp smell of alcohol stung her nose.

"He got caught in one of the emergency locks in maintenance, poor man. I didn't want to mess him about too much, with no proper equipment and no power. Fortunately, that little critter in the tank over there produces a powerful antibiotic."

"Dr. Pennyfeather." Imina took a deep breath. "I have to talk to you." It all tumbled out, higgledy-piggledy, magic makers, whales, webs, and disharmonizing. Dr. Pennyfeather listened, his frown deepening. She was shaking when she finished.

"But m'dear, the evidence indicates that whales haven't much more intelligence than dogs. There must be another explanation."

"Dr. Pennyfeather!" an urgent voice called from the door. "It's Mr. Rossart. I think he's having a stroke. In the cafeteria."

"One moment." Dr. Pennyfeather rose and began to snatch up equipment. "I believe you're telling me the truth as you perceive it," he told Imina, his gentle voice at odds with his flying hands. "I can even believe you're a shaman yourself. I've seen quite a few odd things. I think I can bring myself to believe in some sort of magic. But m'dear, not in whales." He ran from the room.

Imina buried her face in her hands and swore.

"Mr. M'Barra?"

"Draft anyone who isn't an engineer. We need someone with a light at every intersection in the corridors."

"Mr. M'Barra, I have to talk to you. It's important."

"Tell them everyone should head for the auditorium on level fourteen. We'll set up a message board there, and people who are safe can sign in if they don't want to stay. The people at the intersections can collect names, too. If we get a list of the people working in maintenance now, we can start making a master list. Once we know who's here, we can begin to figure out who might be missing."

"Mr. M'Barra!"

His eyes focused on her. "Annis? Your parents are fine. I saw them both not twenty minutes ago." His attention turned. "In a few hours, we'll start searching for anyone who hasn't checked in. We should begin searching the lowest levels right now, before the air gets bad down there. There might be enough convection to keep the carbon dioxide from sinking, but I'm not going to depend on it. If we don't get power back soon, we'll start moving people up."

"Mr. M'Barra, I know what's wrong with the power."

That caught his attention. "You have some idea who the saboteurs are? I know that it's not your friend Ivan's mother. You don't have to worry about that."

"I didn't say I knew who, I said I knew what."

"Annis, no one knows what's wrong with the power yet, not even your father. How could you know?"

"Because I'm a shaman. Like my great-grandmother. She taught me."

Mr. M'Barra frowned. A woman beside him snickered, but he waved her to silence.

Imina clenched her fists. "And what's wrong with the power is magic!"

"I know about your grandmother, but . . . Who's working this magic?"

Everyone was staring at her. Imina's courage failed. She mumbled something.

"Look," said Mr. M'Barra, "I'm really not involved in trying to restore the power. Why don't you tell your parents what you know? All right?"

"But—"

He had already turned away. Imina sighed.

"Mom? Dad?"

It had taken almost half an hour to track down her parents in one of the dozens of small, cramped workshops tucked into the corners of the maintenance sphere. Her mother was holding a hand light for her father, but she spun around when Imina spoke, her expression blazing with relief. "Annis! Thank God. I was worried."

"Signy!" said her father. "The light!"

"Sorry." Her mother turned the beam back to the open panel, but her free arm reached for her daughter.

"I was fine." Imina hugged her.

Her father spared her a glance and a grin. "I told her you had the sense to be all right."

"What are you doing?"

"I'm trying to modify this so it will run off a fuel cell. I want to send an electrical current back through the system and trace it. If we can do that, maybe we can find where the cutoff is."

"Then I was right. The emergency generators aren't working."

"Damned if I can figure that out," her father muttered. "I've got my best people going over every sys-

176

tem on those machines. Don't worry, honey, we've got more than forty hours. As soon as we know how the generators were sabotaged, we'll get them fixed. Then we'll have plenty of time to restore the power."

Imina took a deep breath. "Dad, remember how you always say you should keep an open mind? Well, I need you, both of you, to listen to me. Really listen. You know Grandma Ata was a shaman?"

She told them everything, clearly and in order. Her mother's arm tightened, but Imina kept her eyes on the open panel, a fairy city of crystal and cobweb wires, where her father continued to work with delicate deftness.

"When I saw the pattern the whales were making, I recognized it. It was almost like one Grandma Ata used to confine and intensify magical energy."

Her father's expression was grim, but his hands never stopped. "Could you show us this pattern?"

Imina sighed. "Not without power—though Ivan saw it, too. I should have realized earlier that the whales were the ones doing the magic, but—"

"I have to know! I have a right to know!" The shriek at the door brought Imina and her mother spinning around.

"Light, Signy," her father muttered.

Mrs. Bouchard stood in the doorway, her pleasant face twisted. Lisette clung to her mother's arm. Her mouth was tight, but she wasn't crying. "Please,

Mom, come back to the auditorium. I'm sure it'll be all right. We shouldn't bother them."

Mrs. Bouchard marched up to stand behind Imina's father. "Why isn't the power coming on?"

"We don't know yet. We'll have a better chance of finding out if we aren't interrupted."

"We're going to die." Her voice was rising. "I knew it. I knew it the moment the lights went off. We're all going to die here!"

"Mom, calm down. No one else is panicking. Not even Annis." She glanced at Imina, appraisal and acknowledgment in her cool gaze. Neither of them was panicking. "We need to find some way to help," Lisette went on, "not distract people who're working."

"She's right, Mrs. Bouchard," said Dr. Kent, emerging from the shadows by the door. "You have a very sensible daughter." She smiled at Lisette, laid a friendly hand on Mrs. Bouchard's arm, then rammed a syringe into it.

"What was that? You've poisoned me! You're killing people so you can have all the air!" She burst into tears. It sounded ghastly in the helium-distorted atmosphere.

"Just a tranquilizer to help you calm down," said Dr. Kent soothingly. "Lisette, can you take your mom up and find her a bed?"

Lisette nodded, clutching her mother's shaking

shoulders. "I'll do anything I can."

"Good. I'll come and give her another dose when this stops working. We can keep her out till the whole thing is over, if we have to."

Mrs. Bouchard's sobs were already quieter.

"Just don't let her get near a diving mask, all right? The masks aren't working."

Lisette nodded again and pulled her mother from the room.

"Whew." Dr. Kent slumped against a cabinet. "What a hell of a day."

"Diving masks," Imina's mother said stiffly. "You don't mean people are trying to swim to the surface?"

Dr. Kent nodded, her golden skin muddy gray in the dim light. "One man that we know of. I'm told he grabbed a mask and headed right up. A friend of his tried to catch him. That's how we found out the masks don't work. God help him if he manages to get very far," Dr. Kent shuddered.

Imina's stomach twisted. Decompression sickness. Nitrogen bubbles forming in your body as the pressure of the depths eased, blocking the blood vessels, tearing the muscles, smashing the nervous system, destroying the brain. It was a death that made suffocation look sweet.

"We think there are other people missing," Dr. Kent continued. "When I heard about that man, I stuffed my pockets with syringes, and to hell with good psychiatric practice. I am not going to let a handful of hysterics start a panic down here."

"Dr. Kent," said Imina's father, "I think you ought to talk to Annis."

Imina went rigid.

"Why?" Dr. Kent smiled, but her eyes were suddenly professional, intent. "She's not going to have hysterics. Are you, Annis?"

"No." The shaman belt felt heavy around her neck. *Don't say anything*, she begged her father silently. *Don't do this to me.*

"No hysterics." Her father left the machine and turned to face them. "But she's been telling us an odd story. I think you ought to hear it."

"Traitor." Imina's voice was choked. "You . . ." Her throat closed.

"Annis." Her father reached for her and she leaped back, knocking over a chair. He let his arms fall. His voice shook. "Annis, baby, I love you with all my heart, and if I could come now and talk with you and take care of you, I would, but *I can't come now*. Talk to Dr. Kent, baby. Please." He picked up the hand light Imina's mother had dropped, propped it so he could see, and went back to work.

"I'll come." Imina's mother wiped her face and turned to them, but the tears still poured down.

"Damn you." Imina forced the words past the constriction of her throat. "I hate you. I hate you both." She wouldn't cry. She would not.

"I think it might be better if I talk to Annis alone for a while," said Dr. Kent. Her hands pulled softly on Imina's shoulders. "Come on. Let's go to my office."

Imina stared at her father. His deft hands fumbled, but he was working. He would be working there when Dr. Kent locked her up. He'd still be working, she realized, when the last of the air went. The thought crystallized into a vision of her father, lungs heaving, struggling with some machine while his vision faded and the tools fell from his hands. Like the boy in the stupid poem, he would stay at his post till he died there, because if he didn't restore the power, they would all die. That was why he'd done it.

Imina turned blindly and followed Dr. Kent.

When they reached the office, Dr. Kent handed her a box of tissues. "Cry it out."

"No." Imina blew her nose. "I do have to talk to you. I have to convince someone."

As Imina poured out the story, Dr. Kent's face assumed its professional mask.

"So you see, if someone doesn't do something about the whales, we're going to die here." Imina's fists were clenched. "I understand how crazy it sounds, but I am not crazy. I'm telling the truth, and if someone doesn't believe me, we are going to die."

Dr. Kent pressed her hands over her eyes. They shook slightly. "Full-blown psychosis." It was only a murmur, but Imina heard it. "I should have seen this coming."

"You don't believe me. You think I'm nuts!"

"Annis." Dr. Kent reached across the desk and grasped her hand. She was stronger than she looked. "Annis, I want you to listen, because I refuse to lose you. Fantasies are wonderful things, but you have to keep the fantasy where it belongs. I understand how much your grandmother meant to you. I know how you loved her. But you have to let her go. You have to let go of grief and anger, to hold on to life."

"I know that," Imina wailed. "I have let go. Well, maybe I haven't, but at least I'm trying. This isn't about me, it's about the whales! I'm telling the truth!" She tried to pull her hand back. The doctor's grip tightened. And her pockets were full of syringes.

"Annis, we're going to talk about this a lot, but I don't think now is the right time. There's too much going on that's too scary. So I'm going to take you to the upper levels and find you a room. All right?"

She was going to lock her in. How she would do it with the power off Imina couldn't guess, but she had never underestimated Dr. Kent. "All right." She forced her hand to relax in Dr. Kent's grasp. "I am sort of tired."

Dr. Kent kept hold of her shoulder, but as they

walked down the darkened corridors and Imina made no move to struggle, her grip relaxed a little. Imina showed no sign that she noticed it. Every fiber of her body was ready to run.

They saw the lights first, a mass of hand lights flashing wildly. A mob blocked the corridor in front of them. One of the doors scraped open, and half the crowd spilled into a room.

"Looters?" Imina kept her voice low. There was something menacing about the way the remainder of the mob hovered outside.

"No." Dr. Kent's voice was grim. "I recognize some of them from the meeting. They're looking for Nathalie Simeonov."

"Can they find her?"

"No, Mr. M'Barra has her hidden. I ought to talk to those people. They might hurt someone."

"Talk to them? They're a mob! They're dangerous."

"Not necessarily. I might be able to reason with them." Dr. Kent felt her shiver and looked down. "Not right now. I'll get you somewhere safe first. Come on. We'll go back to the last corridor we passed and go around them."

"Wait a minute!" Imina dragged her to a stop. "What about Ivan? He wasn't with his mother. He was going to try to help with the power. What if they catch him?"

"Ivan is with his mother. They found him in maintenance and sent him to join her. Come on, Annis, I want to get back—"

A shriek rang down the hall. There was a commotion in the lights outside the door, and three men dragged a struggling woman into the corridor.

"What are you doing? She's not the traitor." The surprised voice rose above the hubbub.

Dr. Kent took a step toward the mob. "Oh God." Her hand still gripped, but her attention was no longer focused on Imina. If Imina tried to pull away, Dr. Kent would notice her. But if she relaxed, she might get the chance to escape.

"She's *her* friend. She might know something. Hell, she's probably one of them herself."

"I'm not!" the woman cried. The flashing lights picked out an ugly bruise across her face. "Let me go, damn you. You have no right!"

Imina ordered her muscles to relax. *Forget about me*, she willed. *I'm not important. Forget me.*

Dr. Kent took another step forward. Her grip on Imina's shoulder slackened and fell away.

Imina jumped back and ran down the corridor, away from the mob.

"Annis! Damn." She heard Dr. Kent start to follow her, then the sound of a slap. The woman shrieked. "What do you think you're doing! Let her go." The psychiatrist's voice was filled with cold authority. Imina marveled at Dr. Kent's courage as she ran.

Hunting through the upper levels, Imina avoided the people clustered at the junctions of the winding corridors. She had to find Mr. M'Barra before Dr. Kent found her.

She paused at an intersection. There were men around the corner, speaking softly. Imina listened, but she couldn't tell if any of the voices belonged to Mr. M'Barra. She leaned forward and peered down the hall—two men, opening doors. Checking to see if anyone was trapped? But most of the rooms up here were administrative offices and meeting rooms. Hardly anyone used them.

One of the men flashed his hand light down the hall. She started to pull back, but the beam hit her face, dazzlingly bright. "It's her!"

Imina turned and ran. She heard their feet pounding behind her. Her hand light would show up for hundreds of yards in the dark, so she snapped it off. For an instant she ran blind. Then the beams of the men's hand lights caught her and illuminated the corridor in front of her.

Imina ran. She heard one of them stumble, but she didn't look back. With their lights on her, the floor at their feet would be in near darkness. She turned a corner and shot into the midst of a small crowd. The men chasing her shouted, but she wove through the startled group before they could react. More shouts rang out behind her, and she risked a glance over her shoulder. The men were pushing people aside. She was getting away. A few more minutes and—

She crashed into someone. The force of the collision spun her into the side corridor from which the person had emerged. Imina regained her balance and found herself staring into Lisette's startled eyes.

She turned to run, but the other girl grabbed her with unexpected strength, swung her around, and shoved her through an open door. Imina stumbled and fell. Two hand-light beams struck Lisette, the backwash spilling into the room where Imina lay, and she rolled over and scrambled to kneel in the shadow beside the door.

"A girl." The men were breathing hard. "Black hair. Did you see her?"

"She ran into me." Lisette sounded aggrieved. "She went that way." She pointed down the corridor. "Why are you chasing . . ." She didn't bother to finish. The men were gone. She stepped into the room and slid the door shut.

Imina rose shakily to her feet. "Thanks. I don't know why you did that, but thanks."

"Dr. Kent is asking people to look for you," Lisette said. "She says you're completely over the edge. That you might be dangerous. She says you think what's happening is caused by magic."

"Damn her," Imina muttered. "If everyone starts looking for me, I'll never be able to find him. Do you know where Mr. M'Barra is?"

Lisette shook her head. "He's been running all over. He could be anywhere. He could even be below somewhere. The air isn't too bad yet."

"I have to go." Imina started for the door. "Once they realize they've lost me, they'll probably come back."

"Wait." Lisette opened the door, peering into the corridor. "All right, it's clear. Follow me."

She avoided the main corridors, leading Imina through twisting side passages with an assurance that implied considerable familiarity. They climbed steadily. In the upper levels, elevators replaced the ladders used in maintenance, but with the power off, they had to use the emergency ladders.

"Where are we going?" Imina demanded softly.

"It's a place of mine. I go there when I want to be alone. It's a storage closet between two meeting rooms. No door in the hallway. You can hide there."

"But I can't hide—I have to find Mr. M'Barra."

"You'll never find him," said Lisette. "Not without getting caught. But I can. I'll lead you to him."

"Why?" Imina grabbed Lisette's arm and turned her so that she could see the other girl's face. It was pale, but there was no panic in the blue eyes that looked back at her. "I thought you were with your mother. You don't believe in magic. You don't even like me. Why are you doing this?"

"My mother's asleep." Lisette pulled her arm away. "I can't help her. I can't help the engineers, because I don't know enough. And if I can't do *something*, I'm going to start screaming and pounding the walls. I can help you. Besides, I don't believe Dr. Kent. You're weird, but you're not crazy. And if you aren't crazy, you might be able to help. From what I've been hearing, we're going to need all the help we can get. So come on. It's in here." She went down the hall and through a door. Imina followed.

The door to Lisette's hideout was in the far corner of an undistinguished room, and had been designed to blend with the surrounding panels. Lisette pulled a plastic wedge from her pocket and pried it open.

"It may take a while to find Mr. M'Barra," she said. "Don't do anything stupid. I'll come for you when I've found him." She stood aside and gestured for Imina to go in.

"Thanks." Imina went past her. "Find him as soon as you can. This really is important."

Lisette stared at her, an odd expression on her face.

"What?"

"This room is as high as you can go without getting into the utility shaft. That's all."

She turned and walked away. Imina shrugged and slid the door closed. The darkness was total. She turned on her hand light.

The walls of the small room were covered with holo-posters. On the wall opposite the door, a hawk circled through a clear sky. Next to it, the sun set over a misty beach. Next to that, lightning arced down from violent clouds. This wasn't "a place I go." It was a shrine to the sky. Imina walked around the room. The posters showed the sky in every mood. There wasn't a fashion model among them.

Imina had hardly thought about the sky these last few months, but she remembered it now with a surge of longing. She looked up and caught her breath.

The whole ceiling was covered with a starscape. The Milky Way shone across it in a luminous band. There was no moon. As she watched, a comet streaked across the blackness and faded out. Imina stood, looking up, for a long time.

By the time Lisette returned, she was ready to pull the posters off the wall and tear them to shreds. How many hours could it take to find one man?

"It wasn't just a matter of finding him," Lisette explained. "I had to follow him until he got involved in something that would keep him in the same place for more than two minutes." They were descending steadily, and the air seemed thicker. With Lisette to

189

scout the corridors, they had managed to keep anyone from seeing Imina.

"And you aren't the only one in a hurry," Lisette
added. "I have to get back to my mother. The tranquilizer will wear off soon, and Dr. Kent says she'll
let her stay awake if she can keep calm." They went
down a ladder into a dark hall. Lisette paused a
moment, listening. A rumble of conversation came
from a maintenance bay ahead of them. "He's still
there," she whispered. "Good luck."

Imina nodded, barely noticing Lisette's departure
as she crept closer to the open door. The administrator was standing with a group of men. Two hulking
machines towered beside them, and crated fuel cells
lined the walls.

"I don't understand it," one of the men was saying.
"We've gone over every rod, wire, connector, and
bolt, and they're in perfect working order. They just
don't work!" He punched a button. The big machine
hummed. Then the hum changed pitch, fragmented,
and died.

The silence was grim.

"Now will you listen?" Imina stepped into the
room and winced as the hand lights flashed in her
eyes. They were quickly lowered.

Mr. M'Barra came forward and put his hands on
her shoulders. "You look awful. What's wrong?"

Tears started in Imina's eyes, but she sniffed and

blinked them back. "No one will listen to me. But maybe," she gestured to the big still generators, "maybe you'll listen now. Those machines won't run because magic is being worked on them."

Mr. M'Barra's gaze lifted, and his hands stiffened on her shoulders.

"I know how it sounds," said Imina through gritted teeth. "But look at them. *You* can't explain—" A needle slammed into her arm. She jumped, but Mr. M'Barra was holding her.

"I'm sorry, Annis," said Dr. Kent from behind her. "But I can't deal with this now. Later, when the lights are on—"

"The lights aren't coming on!" Imina cried. She could hear her own voice, thinned by the helium. Even to herself she sounded hysterical. "You fools. If you don't listen to me, we're all going to die. To die!"

The faces around her held weariness, pity, and endurance. They weren't listening. Already she could feel the drug sapping her strength, blackening the edges of her vision. No use. No one would listen. Except maybe . . .

Magic makers, she sent the silent message into the dark with all her will, *You must not do this. You are killing us. Shamans like me. Do not do this. Let us go!*

She was weakening. Her knees buckled, and hands caught her. *Magic makers, hear me, help me. Let us live.*

She had no more strength. The dark closed down.

CHAPTER 10

"I HAVE HEARD THIS CALL BEFORE," *said the Young-one. "There is a Maker amongst them!"*

Consternation rippled around the quorum. The Eldest had summoned only the four needed to make the decision. The Young-one had invited herself.

"Why are you not lending power to the spell-that-silences-the-idiot-song?" he asked. "Is that not your duty now?"

"I have information that may influence the decision," said the Young-one. "Don't you understand? There is a Maker calling us, begging us to stop the attack. If they breed Makers-of-Magic, they are a people. We must not do this!"

"A people?" said a Far-seer. "They are not people."

"How do we know?" demanded the Young-one.

"This is a waste of time," said the Eldest. "Young-one, return to the spell."

"How can you say that? If they are a people, we are working the blackest of magics."

"They have invaded the world. They refused to go when we warned them. With the death of the Singer, they broke a truce that lasted for generations. Even if they are a people, it cannot be allowed to make a difference. We will do what we must."

<hr />

Something was wrapped around Imina's chest, and it was too tight. She squirmed sleepily, trying to free herself.

"That's the way, m'dear," said Dr. Pennyfeather. "Wake up now."

She pushed the blankets away, and cold air flowed over her, but her chest was still tight. It was the air that was wrong—heavy, stifling. She opened her eyes. A night sky, blazing with stars. No, a holo-poster. Lisette's place. Ivan sat at her feet. He looked tired. Dr. Pennyfeather knelt beside her. Why was she lying on the floor? Memory flooded back. She tried to sit up. Mistake.

"Give it a few minutes, m'dear," said Dr. Pennyfeather, pressing her back. "I'm a wonderful doctor, but not a miracle worker."

"The air." Imina pressed her hands to her throbbing forehead. "How long do we have?"

"About six hours," Ivan said.

Imina heard the effort he made to sound calm, but she didn't care. "Six hours! You let me sleep? What took you so long? Ivan!" She tried to sit up again, but Dr. Pennyfeather stopped her. "You'd better hide. The mob is looking for you."

"That," said Ivan, "is part of what took so long."

"But you should hide."

"Stop fussing. Dr. Kent disbanded the mob, and the leaders are under arrest. In a way, it was a good thing. While I was waiting with my mother, I had time to think, and I realized that . . . something I couldn't explain was affecting the equipment. Then I had to confirm my theory. I found a tuning fork—"

"A tuning fork?" asked Imina. "Where?"

Ivan glared at her. "I found a tuning fork, and I tried it. Watch." He took a small metal Y out of his pocket and rapped the floor. Its hum changed to a screech and died within two seconds. "Some sort of sonic damper. At least that's how it acts. But there's no technology in the world that will do that on this scale. Especially not in the hands of the Unificationists, because my mother would know about it. My first thought then was to find you and ask if . . . if it really could be magic."

"That took you more than thirty hours?"

"It took me a while to figure out it couldn't be mechanical, all right? I'm a scientist. Magic doesn't leap to my mind as a probable cause."

"And then," put in Dr. Pennyfeather, "he had to find out what had happened to you. You can sit up now, m'dear. Then he had to find and convince me, because I could counteract the drug Dr. Kent gave you. She'd decided to keep you out for the duration."

"How come you believed him when you wouldn't believe me?" Imina demanded.

"Because he was carrying the proof in his pocket," said Dr. Pennyfeather.

Why hadn't *she* thought of trying something like that? Imina grimaced and rubbed her face, trying to scrub away the last of the drug-induced sleep.

"And because I'd had time to do some thinking," the doctor continued. "You see, m'dear, I didn't believe you were crazy. And if you weren't crazy, I had to consider that you might be right. You could say that the two of you convinced me together."

"And then," said Ivan, "we had to get rid of your mother."

"What do you mean?"

"She's been sitting with you," said Dr. Pennyfeather, "while you slept."

"She wouldn't even listen to us," Ivan added. "She just sat there and stroked your hair, as if she were deaf."

Imina swallowed. "How did you get her to go?"

"Lisette told her your father needed help. He's given up on the main system. He's building a new generator, from parts that couldn't have been tampered with. We told her that most of the engineers had gone to be with their families, and that he really needed her. Then we smuggled you in here. She may come looking for you, so we'd better hurry."

"Right." Imina tried to take a deep breath. It didn't work very well. "What are we going to do?"

There was a long pause. "We were hoping you'd have an idea," said Dr. Pennyfeather.

Imina's stomach clenched.

"I have an idea," said Ivan. "You know how you shielded the skid when we were attacked?"

Imina nodded.

"Could you shield one of the emergency generators? In nine days the supply ship will arrive."

"Against power like that? Nine days? You're kidding." Imina gestured toward the dark sea. "Without help I couldn't shield it for nine minutes. But if you chanted for me and if I shielded it for a few hours, then rested a few hours and shielded it again, could we restore the air?"

"No." Ivan shook his head. "Most of the problem is getting rid of carbon dioxide that's built up in the last thirty hours. It will take almost that long, running the equipment continuously, to get the air quality up to normal. You might extend our time by a few hours, but that's all."

Imina stood and began to pace. She knew she was using up more oxygen, but she couldn't sit still. "What about help? If we shield a generator, we can run the telio, send a distress call. The coastal patrol could run the whales off."

"We can run the telio on fuel cells," Ivan told her. "The sound waves die about a hundred yards from the habitat. The . . . the spell stops them, I guess. But even if we could get a signal out, no one could get to us. The storm's too bad. No surface craft could make it."

"What about submersibles? Won't someone realize we're in trouble when they don't hear from us?"

"We thought of that, but it was eleven at night when the power went off. They won't have realized that we weren't transmitting till midmorning, maybe afternoon. Then they'd check their equipment. And yesterday afternoon, the nearest submersible craft was more than two days away."

"And even if they came in time, the whales would shut them down, too," Imina concluded.

"M'dear, about the whales. Are you quite sure?"

"Positive," said Imina. "What about weapons? Could we drive them off ourselves?"

Ivan snorted. "The closest thing we have to a

weapon is the sonic shark repeller on the diving belts. It has a range of about five yards. And they seem to be better at sonics than we are."

"Could we make weapons?"

"Ones that would work without power? We might do something with chemical explosives, but they'd have to be used at point-blank range. Even if we could make enough to arm all the people in the habitat and convince them to do it, how could they swim out to the whales? The masks don't work. Not to mention the fact that the whales would just swim away from us."

"All right, what's your idea? I've had two. It's your turn."

"M'dear, about the whales. Why don't you just talk to them?"

"Talk to them?"

Dr. Pennyfeather nodded. "I seem to remember that Inuit shamans could communicate with animals."

"With animals, yes. But they haven't got much of a mind. All you have to do with animals is convince them to want what you want. These are magic makers. They're intelligent. They're stronger than I am."

"If you're all magic makers, you'd have something in common."

"I'm not really a shaman," said Imina. "The spirits haven't chosen me. And when I tried to talk to the whales before, when I didn't know who they were, they wouldn't answer."

"Maybe you need to try again, now that you know."

"I think the spell they're casting at the habitat would keep my spell from reaching them," said Imina. "Besides, mind-speaking is always harder over a long distance. And the longer and more complex the message is, the greater the chance of it being distorted, and this one would have to be awfully complex."

Neither of the others said anything.

Imina's hands clenched. "You want me to go out. You want me to swim out there, and call the whales." Her voice failed.

"You're the only one who can shield a diving mask," said Ivan. "You're also the only one who can speak to the whales. Therefore, you're the only one who can convince them to leave us alone."

"I can't even convince white people to listen to me. How am I supposed to convince whales?"

"You persuaded Ivan," said Dr. Pennyfeather. "You persuaded me."

"But you're human!"

"They're mammals. They're intelligent. And they're shamans, of a sort."

"But what if I can't reach them? What if I fail? What if they kill me?"

"Then you're no worse off than you are now," said Ivan. "Are you?"

The silence stretched for a long time.

"All right," said Imina. "How do I get out?"

"Lisette's standing guard on an open access two corridors over. She'll scout for us. She's on our side."

"Just what I need. Lisette on my side."

Imina slid the amulet inside her skin suit and let it rest against her chest. The charms on her grandmother's shaman belt clicked as she tucked it into a waterproof pouch. *Oh, Grandma, lend me your wisdom now.*

Ivan, Dr. Pennyfeather, and Lisette sat as she had told them, in a semicircle, hand lights on the floor before them. The access opened into a small alcove off the main corridor. With everybody's lights pointed at the ceiling, the corners were lost in shadow. One by one, she gathered their eyes . "I want you to chant. Like this: '*Aja-ja, aja-ja.*'"

It took all their power to create the shield spell, but once it was properly cast, Imina found it fairly easy to maintain. She could swim and protect her mask with no trouble. But she had to get outside the web before she could call the whales. At least the air was good. She flashed her light around, hoping to attract Stupid, but saw no sign of him.

Imina chose a compass heading at random and swam away from the habitat. She knew she should be trying to think of arguments that would convince the whales to stop their attack, but her mind was blank. How did you convince a whale to do anything? She couldn't even convince her parents that she was sane. Though she might have, if she'd thought to use a tuning fork. Imina scowled and swam on.

The sea floor that showed in the cone of light beneath her gave her no sense of the distance she covered, but she felt the cessation of the spell like the release of a giant hand. She stopped then and floated in the water, trying to relax. She felt oddly free.

The surface was three days' decompression away. You might do it in two and a half, in an emergency. There were extra fuel cells in her diving belt to power the mask. Once the whales left, she could swim back to the habitat and rise beside the utility shaft. Five feet per hour, no more than sixteen hours' decompression in a twenty-four-hour day was the rule. She could tie her belt rope to the shaft when she slept, so she wouldn't drift. The thirst would be awful, but the generators at the surface produced fresh water as well as power. If she made it to the top, she'd still be alive when the storm broke and rescue arrived.

And in the dark of the habitat, everyone would be dead. She thought of her father, struggling to build another generator. Her mother, holding a light for him. Ivan and Dr. Pennyfeather, waiting by the access, trusting her. But it wasn't just her parents and friends, it was all of them. Even Lisette. Even the ones she didn't know. The habitat had become her community. She laughed suddenly, inside the mask. They were her tribe.

She swam until she found a shattered light, to which she anchored her belt rope so she wouldn't drift up or back into the spell. She switched her belt light from beam to glow, and a circle of light bloomed in the water around her. Then she closed her eyes. She had to relax her muscles deliberately, one by one, as she chanted the *aja*s.

The summoning that rose from the depths of her being wasn't like the frantic cry to the unknown she had broadcast before. It was a message from shaman to shaman. She summoned them as if she had the right to do so.

Whales, I name you.
Whales, I summon you.
As my ancestors did reverence to your spirits,
So do I now.
I would speak with you.
I would speak with you.
In the name of the magic we wield.
In the name of the life that is the source of all magic

I would speak with you.
I would speak with you.

"We are here." The mind-voice was a rumble of power that shook her bones.

Imina opened her eyes and gasped. Huge shapes loomed in the grayness at the edge of her light. One of them was less than ten feet from her, the end of its long body lost in the dimness. A single alien eye watched her from the midst of its great bulk. A wave of terror swept over Imina, numbing her mind. She hadn't really believed they'd come. And she'd never imagined how *big* they were.

A flicker of contempt for her fear, for her smallness, reached her. She couldn't tell which of them it came from.

"Yes, I am afraid." She sent the answer out blindly at them all. "But I must speak with you anyway."

She'd come out of the trance, but the channel of communication remained open. She felt their responses to her defiant statement. Anger, contempt, amusement, and from somewhere, a wave of admiration and curiosity. She turned, looking for it, but the mind-voices were directionless.

"We understand that you wish to speak to us." There was a dry note in the rumble of power. "And we are obliged to listen. Any Maker-of-Magic will be heard by the council, even though you are our enemy. What do you want to say?"

Imina took a deep breath. Ridiculous, since she spoke with her mind and will instead of her lungs, but she couldn't help it. "I don't want to be your enemy."

"Then why did you come from above-the-world, and summon the warm-ice-reef and the shoal-of-lights, and break the truce-that-has-lasted-for-generations?"

"Uh, will you tell me about the truce? Your side of it, I mean. Because sometimes, when two groups have been in conflict, they see things in a different way, right?"

"You speak truly. But why take the time for this? The truce is broken."

"Please. Perhaps it can be mended. And I have a great need to understand about your . . . people."

"Eldest." It was a different mind-voice, less powerful but suffused with . . . energy? interest? life? "We have no need for haste. Why not give the small Maker the knowledge she seeks?"

"I have need . . . No, forget it. Tell me about the truce." Imina hoped it wouldn't take more than five hours.

"The Far-seer called a council," the power rumble—the Eldest—began. "She said that the things-that-move-above-the-world were hunting us beyond reason. That we were falling out of harmony with the world, and that unless we found a spell to stop them, our people would be no more."

The other whales joined their voices with the power voice, and somehow the story became a poem. But it wasn't even rhythmic. The whales were singing. The bizarre squeaks and shrieks that so many scientists had failed to analyze were not words, but an addition to the mind-voice that supplied— emphasis? depth? feeling? Imina wasn't sure. But hearing it through the minds of the whales, it made speech into poetry, into song. No wonder the scientists had never figured it out.

She had to struggle with some of the concepts, but the gist was clear. They had created a spell that stopped machines, and once they began to use it, the hunting stopped. When no thing-that-moves-above-the-world had slain a whale for a full generation, the truce had been declared.

It took her many verses to realize that the thing-that-moves-above-the-world were humans, and their ships. She was still trying to grasp the implications when the song ended.

"I . . . I thank you for telling me this," Imina faltered as they fell silent. "I understand much more than I did. But the truce was that the killing stop. How has it been broken? We haven't killed anyone."

A current of anger and grief coursed through the

water around her. "The Singer is dead." It was a new voice, full of sorrow. "All his power lost. Your invisible-spell-that-touches wrapped about his body and crushed him. Does that not break the truce?" Another wave of anger reached her, and it took her several seconds to understand.

"The whale that was caught in the power surge. We didn't intend for that to happen. It wasn't by our will that the whale, uh, the Singer died. He was trying to tamper with our spell, and it disrupted the spell's balance. That's what killed him. We didn't want him to die. Not at all."

"And those who maintained this spell could not control it?" Another voice, sharp with sarcasm.

Imina had given up trying to match voices with the huge bodies that drifted at the edges of her light. She was vaguely aware that they came and went. Surfacing for air?

"No," she said. "If it had happened more slowly they might have, but they weren't aware of the Singer's meddling until it was too late."

"That is a lie. Anyone knows instantly when a spell is tampered with."

"No," said Imina. "I'm telling the truth."

"She is," the Eldest confirmed. "She has not enough skill in speaking to lie without my knowing it."

Imina was glad she hadn't tried to lie before she

206

found that out. "The force nets the Singer disrupted weren't really a spell." How to explain machines? Whales didn't even use tools. "They were another kind of magic," she fumbled on. "We call them machines. We do control them, but in a different way. We can't tell if they're being disturbed until it's happened. I swear to you, the Singer's death was an accident brought on by his own spell. We didn't kill him."

"She speaks the truth," said the Eldest. "But his power is lost to us."

"But the truce hasn't been broken," Imina argued. "Not by us. You have killed. You killed Mr. Wu. And by silencing the machines, the idiot-songs, you are killing us all! *You* are breaking the truce!"

The silence felt uneasy. Imina's skin prickled. But when the Eldest spoke, his voice was thoughtful. "Why didn't you leave when we warned you?"

"Because we didn't understand," said Imina. "We knew there was trouble, but we didn't know who caused it, or why. You see, we never knew that you are a people, too."

The wave of emotion that came from the whales was too mixed to sort out. The ripple of comment that accompanied it was clearer. *The things-that-moved-above-the-world were not people. That was ridiculous. They sang only the one-note idiot-songs. How do you know that, Weather-shaper? We know nothing about them.* Arguments were beginning.

"Silence." It was the Eldest. They obeyed him instantly. "This is irrelevant. The question is not whether they are a people, the question is whether they go."

There was no movement among the dark forms, but Imina could tell when the Eldest's attention focused on her. "We will accept that the Singer's death was an accident, but it was an accident caused by your presence here, where you do not belong. If we cease the spell-that-silences-the-idiot-songs, will you go? Not only you, but all your kind, from all the warm-ice-reefs you have summoned into the world?"

Imina took a deep breath. "We can't."

Outrage, anger, force-them-out.

"Please," she cried. "Hear me. In my world, above-the-world, the Unificationists . . ." Politics. Crop virus. The very concept of agriculture, of planting things to harvest and eat. Eating plants. Damn.

"A group of evil magic makers," Imina began again, "worked a terrible spell above-the-world. It's destroying all that we eat, and we cannot stop it . . ."

A brooding silence hovered when she finished.

"I see your need," said the Eldest. "But to let you invade the world itself, to eat all the small-life and throw the world out of harmony."

"We won't throw the world out of harmony,"

Imina promised. "That's what the habitat, the warm-ice-reef, is for. To create more food for the small life, so that even though we take more, more will still be there."

"I understand you," said the Eldest, "though you express it badly. But it seems your kind are unable to keep your own places in harmony. Should we trust you with the world?"

"You have no choice," said Imina. "If you drive us out, we'll be forced to end the truce. We must be here, or our people will die. And we will not permit that. Others will learn who's destroying the warm-ice-reefs. You'll be hunted again, from above-the-world where your spells won't reach. And if we must, we'll destroy you."

Their anger was almost tangible.

"We wouldn't want to," said Imina. "When we hunted you before, we didn't know you were a people. To destroy you now would be a terrible thing. But if it were the only way to survive, we would. We would grieve, but we'd do it."

"Your kind would commit evil simply to survive?" There was a shock in the mind-voice. "You are not people."

"We are people," said Imina forcefully. "We're different, but we are people. And our evil, this will to survive, is also our strength. If we're forced to fight, we'll win."

"If," said the Eldest, "you can destroy us before your food runs out."

The weight of their determination pressed against her. These were a people who would die, Imina realized, before committing an act they regarded as evil. Only the ultimate violence—killing every last one of them—would defeat them. If it could be done before the food ran out. What could you offer a creature to whom life meant so little?

"We'd rather not fight," said Imina desperately. "We'll do everything we can to keep this world in harmony. If you help us, surely we can succeed."

"Why should we help you?"

"So that both our people might survive! Isn't that reason enough?"

"To risk the harmony of which we are the guardians? No."

"There will be no harmony if we're forced to fight! What will become of your world, if no guardians are left? You have to let go," said Imina. "You have to let go of the past if you're going to survive."

"So you would invade our world, and take of it, and give nothing back but threats? No, Small-Maker, I will not accept so dishonorable a bargain. We will not cease the spell. You may not stay."

"What could we give you?" Imina cried. "We understand giving value for value, but we're so different! What can we offer that you'll accept?"

"Nothing that you have, Small-Maker. For you are not a people."

"Among our own kind," said one of the voices that had spoken before, "we trade stories. Do you understand this?"

"Stories?" Imina shook her head. "You mean, made-up stories?"

"Stories to pass the long migrations. Stories that sing to the spirit and give joy to the generations. Stories that speak to the soul of what we are. These are the mark of a people. Do you have stories?"

"Don't be absurd, Young-one," a voice chimed in. "They could not."

"But we do have stories!" Imina cried. "We have thousands of stories. Millions of stories! Stories the likes of which you've never heard!"

"How many stories?" Flickers of interest came from all directions. Imina stifled a giggle. They cared nothing for a threat of war to the death, but . . .

"Lifetimes of stories." She tried to put it into terms they might comprehend. "More stories than we could tell you in many generations."

Interest, doubt, curiosity. So many stories had already been told, new ones were rare. What would these alien stories be like?

"Prove it," said the Eldest.

"What?"

"Prove to us that your kind have stories, that they might be worth trading for. Tell us one of your stories."

"Uh, sure." Imina's mind went blank. She knew hundreds of Inuit stories, but they were so rooted in the Inuit culture that even white people didn't understand them. Sometimes *she* didn't understand them. A whale would never get the point. She needed something with universal meaning. *Hamlet*? Marriage customs. Inheritance of property. Poison. She needed something simple, something even a child could understand. A thought struck her, and this time she did giggle. But it was simple. It had meaning. Her father had shown her that. Maybe even universal meaning. She knew it by heart. And the whales were waiting.

"'The boy stood on the burning deck.'" Another giggle rose in Imina's throat. She struggled to keep it out of her mind-voice. "'Whence all but him had fled . . .'"

She had to tell it twice. Once she'd gotten around the difficulties of ship and fire, the rest of the concepts followed easily.

"It is too short," said the Eldest when she finished. "And what of the boy's mother? Where was she?"

"It doesn't say." Imina tried to put her weariness out of her mind. "I chose a short one deliberately, so I wouldn't have to explain too much. We have stories it would take days to tell you, but you'd have to learn my people's customs and history before you could understand them."

"You sing the history of your people?"

"Of course," said Imina. "Don't all people?"

"And you will give us your history, and your stories, if we accept your presence in the world?"

"And your help, to keep it in harmony. And perhaps, we would like to learn your history, and your stories, too. If you'll share them."

"It must be considered," said the Eldest. "But I think this bargain might be accepted. There remains only one debt—the power of the Singer, now gone from our councils."

"I . . . I'm a magic maker. Could I help you?"

"Not fair exchange." The voice of the Eldest was almost gentle. "You are young in power, Small-Maker, and untrained. The Singer was strong and skilled."

"More stories?"

"Only power can be offered for power."

"But I'm the only magic maker I know!"

"What of the Maker-spirit with you? She has a Singer's mind. And she is old and strong, though bound and silent."

"The Maker-spirit." Blood drained from Imina's face. She gripped the pouch that held the shaman belt. "No. She is my grandmother. When I've learned enough, I'll be able to summon her spirit and have her with me again, to teach and counsel me. No."

"Would you keep her power bound, unused, forever? We have great need of Singers, for without a Singer to command and focus the spell, the Makers cannot join their power in even the smallest circle. You have a Singer's spirit. And we have need of Singers."

"You don't understand. When someone dies, the spirit divides into two parts. One goes away. The other, which is bound by the name, stays as a ghost until that name is given to a child. Then the spirit joins the child's spirit to form a new soul. My grandmother bound both parts of her spirit to her name. If you break that binding, the conscious part of her, the part that knows magic, will be gone. Only her power will remain. And besides, we can't break the binding. I don't know how."

"You underestimate our knowledge, Small-Maker." A new voice. Amused. "What do you think a Ghostspeaker does? The part of the spirit that remains is the part that will turn a Maker-born child into a Singer, when we give it your grandmother's name. You have only to tell us the name."

"But she would be gone. No."

"Power for power." The Eldest's voice was final. "Or the debt is unpaid. We will not bargain with those who do not pay their debts."

"But it wasn't me who killed the Singer."

It didn't matter. It was a debt incurred by the presence of her kind. If her kind were to continue here, it must be paid. An illogical, alien logic.

Her kind. Her people. Her tribe.

Fumbling, she opened the pouch. The belt's soft leather was slippery in the water. She tried to throw it from her, but it moved only a few inches. "Her name was Naneruut. It means little flame."

The whales started a spell. She felt the power building, focused on the belt before her, but she paid it no heed. Was this the destiny her grandmother had waited for? Imina didn't know and could hardly bring herself to care.

The power lashed out. Every charm on the belt exploded into fragments of bone and ivory.

A wave of her grandmother's presence, a pulse of triumph and joy, engulfed Imina and passed on, and she cried out in protest at its passing.

"Power has paid for power." Even the Eldest sounded weary. "We will give the name of Naneruut to one of our children, and we will come for the first of your stories. Soon."

Water buffeted her as the whales swam away, but Imina didn't care. She was crying inside the mask, silently, fiercely. Her face was wet and she couldn't wipe it. It itched. She sniffed hard and blinked. A whale swam before her. Black and white. A killer whale. She cringed.

"I am the Young-one." The mind-voice sounded hesitant. Almost shy. "I spoke several times, but you wouldn't have noticed me."

"What do you want?" Imina tried to make it sound polite, but she was too tired. She swam down and unfastened the rope. She felt as if the habitat was a million unswimmable miles away.

"You are weary." The mind-voice was sympathetic. "And you wish to return to the warm-ice-reef. You were attached to the bottom. If you could attach yourself to me, perhaps I could take you there?"

Imina sniffed again. "In exchange for what?"

"We don't always demand an exchange." The voice was embarrassed. It was hard to associate that expressive voice with the expressionless bulk before her, but Imina no longer feared it. "I would take you, simply because you are tired and you grieve."

It was the only ride she was likely to be offered. Imina swam forward and grasped the whale's dorsal fin. She'd seen pictures of people doing this, but had never expected to do it herself.

"That feels strange." The Young-one began to swim. "But I don't mind it. How does it feel to you?"

"Strange," said Imina. The Young-one began to swim, faster than a skid. The water dragged at her, and the muscular body surging beneath her was incredible. "But I like it. What is it you want?"

"I said I asked no exchange." The voice was indignant.

"I know, but you're not a good enough speaker to lie, either. I can feel you not saying something."

"It's just . . . I have so many questions!" the Young-one burst out. "In your story for instance. What, exactly, was the monster that was eating the shell-that-you-move-about-in? Why was it so hungry? And could no one slay it, or distract it with other prey?"

Imina began to laugh. "I'll try to answer your questions," she said, "though it isn't going to be easy. But for this, *I* want something in exchange."

"What?" The Young-one sounded cautious, but willing. Almost eager.

"Will you teach me magic? The magic of your people?"

"Of course," said the Young-one cheerfully. "Anyone would do that, and the Ghost-speaker says you are ready for the spirits' choosing. All who have the power to be Makers-of-Magic must be taught. Would you like to begin now? In exchange for answers?"

"Not now." Could the whales' Ghost-speaker know what the spirits would do? She was almost too tired to care.

"Tomorrow, then? I mean, when the world has

darkened and lightened again."

"I know what tomorrow means."

"Then I will come when you call me. And now," the Young-one stopped swimming, "we are here." They'd stopped just short of the lights of the habitat.

Imina released the Young-one and drifted in the water.

"Can you return from here by yourself?" the Young-one asked.

"Sure," said Imina. "I'm just—" Bump! The blow struck her between the shoulder blades, shoving her forward. Bump. Bump. Bump. "Stupid!"

"I will leave you," the Young-one's voice held a smile, "since I see you'll be well escorted."

Imina had bid the Young-one farewell and swam into the light before she realized what it meant. The power was back.

The air in the alcove was still stuffy, but Imina barely noticed it. Her father pulled her from the water. Her mother's arms were around her. She was crying and babbling. Then her father's arms closed around both of them.

Dr. Pennyfeather reached in and deftly stripped off Imina's mask. His eyes sparkled. "We broke out the champagne for you when the lights came on," he told her. "Well done, m'dear."

The corridor behind him was crowded with agitated people. Imina caught a glimpse of Ivan, talking earnestly to Mr. M'Barra. He spared a moment to flash her a wide, triumphant smile.

"I went back and you weren't there," her mother was saying. "I tried to find you." Her voice quivered. Imina felt her shaking, and tears rose in her own eyes. Her father's arms tightened.

"I'm sorry," Imina faltered. "I didn't mean to frighten you. It was the whales."

Her mother released her just enough to see her face. "Whales, Annis?"

"Yes." Imina wiped her eyes. "I have a lot to tell you. But before I start, Mom, I really hate the name Annis. Would you call me Imina? Please?"